THE CHRISTMAS PAWDCAST

A NOVELLA

EMILY MARCH

EMILY MARCH BOOKS

Published in the United States by Emily March Books.

www.EmilyMarch.com

ISBNs 978-1-942002-57-4 (paperback) 978-1-942002-56-7 (ebook)

ACKNOWLEDGMENTS

My sincere thanks to my editor Rose Hilliard. It's been such a joy to work with you over the years on my Eternity Springs projects. Here's to many more to come!

Register for Emily March's newsletter and never miss a new Celebrate Eternity Springs release!

CHAPTER 1

DALLAS, TEXAS

"Carol of the Bells" drifted from the sound system and blended with the laughter of the holiday party guests who were taking their leave. Mary Landry worked to keep the smile on her face as she hugged and cheek-kissed and waved goodbyes to the stragglers. She had enjoyed the party, and she was thrilled that so many invited guests had attended. But seriously, would these people never go home? She still had so much to do! How could it possibly already be December twentieth?

"Tonight was so much fun," bubbled a wedding planner from Plano, her blue eyes sparkling with champagne. "Landry and Lawrence Catering throws the best party of the season, year in and year out. Thanks so much for inviting us!"

"I'm so glad you could join us." Mary graciously accepted the woman's enthusiastic hug and glanced up at her date. "Shall I call an Uber for y'all?"

"We're good," he said. "I'm the designated driver tonight, but I can't say I missed the booze. Your non-alcoholic eggnog was killer."

"Mary is the best chef in Dallas," the wedding planner declared. "Restaurants are always trying to lure her into their kitchens."

"Mary! Great party!" A venue manager sailed toward them, which helped ease the first couple out the door. "I don't know what tweak you made to your mac-and-cheese recipe, but it made the exquisite simply divine."

She hadn't changed a thing. "Thank you, Liz."

"You gonna share your recipe?"

"Nope. Trade secrets."

"Dang it. Although my waistline and arteries both thank you for that. Merry Christmas, Mary."

"Merry Christmas."

Finally, almost an hour after the party had been scheduled to end, Mary's business partner Eliza Lawrence shut the door behind the last guest. She gave her long brown hair a toss and flourished her arms like a game show hostess. "We are so freaking awesome!"

Mary laughed. "Yes, we are."

"I do believe tonight even topped last year's party, which I didn't think would be possible."

"Everything went like clockwork—except getting guests to depart."

Eliza waved her hand dismissively. "That's the sign of a successful event. You know that."

Mary nodded. It was why their Christmas event was the one party of the year where Eliza, the logistics director of their business, loosened her timeline.

"Everyone raved about the food as usual," Eliza continued, "but the shrimp balls were a particular hit. You outdid yourself with those, Mary. The vendors who were here tonight are going to talk them up to their clients. We'll be up to our elbows in shrimp all next year."

"I figured they'd be a hit. Nothing has topped my maple mac-and-cheese, though. I think that was all gone by nine o'clock."

"The Landry and Lawrence classic." Eliza sighed happily. "You ready for a glass of champagne? I built time for champagne into our schedule. The cleanup crew doesn't arrive for forty minutes."

"I'm more than ready." Mary's thoughts returned to her to-do list, and she winced. "Mind drinking it in my office? I need to finish my dad's gift before I head home tonight."

Eliza chastised her with a look.

"I know. I know."

Her partner reached out and gave Mary a quick hug. "I'll grab a bottle and glasses and meet you in your office on one condition."

Mary's mouth twisted in a crooked smile. "What's that?"

"Change your clothes before you break out the hot glue gun. I don't want to be taking you to the ER with third-degree boob burns five days before Christmas."

Mary snorted.

"I think I heard almost as many comments on how great you looked tonight as I heard about how fantastic the shrimp balls tasted. It's a spectacular dress, Mar. I'm glad you decided to show off your curves for a change. Emerald is your color. It brings out your eyes. I swear, when Travis arrived and got a look at you, I thought he was going to swallow his tongue."

"Because I'm wearing last year's Christmas gift." Mary fingered the teardrop garnet pendant that nestled against her breasts. "He accidentally left it off the list of things he asked me to return when he dumped me."

Eliza wrinkled her nose. "If I said it once, I said it a thousand times. The man is a dewsh. I know we couldn't cut him

3

from the guest list because he does own three wedding venues in the Metroplex, but I honestly didn't think he'd have the nerve to show up with her in tow."

"Oh, I knew they'd be here." That's why she'd made such an effort with her outfit tonight.

"Well, you definitely won tonight's skirmish. Raylene sailed in here dressed in her slinky silver sequins, holding her nose in the air and flashing her rock, but you put her in her place without so much as a 'Bless your heart,' just by being gracious."

"She's a beautiful woman."

"And you're a natural red-headed pagan goddess—who will find somebody worthy of you. Trust me, you dodged a bullet by getting rid of that creep."

Emotion closed Mary's throat, and tears stung her eyes. How was it that Eliza always knew just the right thing to say? While she'd put Travis Trent behind her, and she hadn't cried over him in over five months, seeing him tonight hadn't been easy. No woman enjoyed seeing her ex parade her replacement around in front of her. Especially not in her own place of business. Clearing her throat, Mary tried to lighten the subject by saying, "I was aiming for sexy Santa's helper."

"Honey, I wouldn't be surprised to find a dozen men in red suits and white beards lined up outside our door when we leave here tonight."

Mary laughed. What would she do without her best friend? "Oh, Eliza. I do love you."

"I love you, too. Now go cover up that fabulous rack so you can finish your dad's gift. I'm going to change, too, and then I'll grab the bubbly and meet you in your office."

Ten minutes later, armed with a hot glue gun and wearing jeans, a sweatshirt, and her favorite sneakers, Mary put the finishing touches on the Daddy-Daughter scrapbook she'd made for her father. It had long been a Landry family tradition between her parents and two siblings to exchange handmade gifts at Christmas. With her brother and sister both married, the practice had expanded to include spouses and Mary's two nephews and three nieces. Of course, she bought the little ones toys, too, but handmade gifts where the ones that mattered for the adults.

Eliza strolled into her office, carrying two crystal flutes in her right hand and a green bottle in her left. She set the glasses on Mary's desk and went about the business of opening the champagne. "Sorry I took so long. John called to grovel about missing the party, so I let him do it even though I totally support his job. I knew what I was in for when I fell for an obstetrician."

"Did his patient have her babies?"

"She did. Mama and triplets are doing great."

"Excellent."

Eliza filled two glasses with the sparkling wine, handed one to Mary, then raised her glass in a toast. "Merry Christmas, BFF."

"Merry Christmas. I hope you and John have a fabulous time in Hawaii."

"How can we not? Ten days of sun and sand, just the two of us, totally unplugged? It'll be heaven."

"The unplugged part sounds like heaven," Mary agreed.

"You're such a traditionalist, Mary."

"And unapologetic about it. For me, Christmas wouldn't be Christmas without all the trappings. I want family around me, bubble lights on the tree, and carols on the sound system. I want cookies to decorate and big fluffy bows on gifts. I want midnight mass and hot apple cider and 'It's a Wonderful Life' and sleigh rides. And I want snow!"

Eliza clinked her glass with Mary's. "And this is the

difference between a girl born and raised in south Texas and one who grew up in the Rocky Mountains. So, when are you planning to leave for Colorado?"

"With any luck, first thing tomorrow morning." Mary sipped her champagne, then set it down. She checked the finishing touch on the scrapbook with her fingertip. The miniature fishing creel placed at the corner of a twenty-year-old photo of her father fishing with his three children in Rocky Mountain National Park was nice and dry. It was safe to close the book. Mary needed to wrap it and the two hard-cover novels containing the handmade gift IOU's she was giving her brother and sister before she headed home. Her sibs understood her busy season and would be happy with better-late-than-never, thank goodness.

"In other good news, I finally found a dog sitter for Angel. Jason Elliott told me tonight he'd take her. He just needs to clear it with his roommate. He said he'd call me tonight if there was a problem, and my phone hasn't rung."

On cue, Mary's cell phone rang.

It lay pushed to the side of her desk in its seasonal decorative Santa case. Her ring tone of choice for December was "White Christmas," and for the first time in Mary's life, the sound of Bing Crosby's voice didn't make her happy. She closed her eyes and whimpered a little as she reached to answer. "Hello?"

Two and a half minutes later, she disconnected the call, buried her head in her hands, and groaned.

Eliza set a champagne flute in front of her. "No room at Jason's inn, either, I take it?"

"No. Jason was my last hope. There's no other option. I've called every vet, every boarding facility, pet hotel, and pet sitter within fifty miles. Everything is full and has a waitlist.

Nobody is offering me any hope that Angel will find a bed for Christmas."

Eliza winced. She took a sip of her drink and then pursed her lips and pondered a moment. "You asked Sarah?"

"Yes. And Linda, April, José, Kiley, Kenisha, Sam, Father Tom, Reverend Jenkins, Officer Larimer…"

"The butcher, the baker, and the candlestick maker?"

"Them, too."

"I'm sorry, sweets. You'd know I'd help if John and I weren't leaving for Hawaii tomorrow. I suppose it wouldn't be kind of me to say I told you so when you said yes to Wags and Walks?"

Mary chastised her partner with a look.

Eliza lifted her champagne in a toast. "Honey, you know I love dogs as much as anybody, and I think the work you do for Wags and Walks Rescue qualifies you for sainthood. But that dog…"

"She's an angel," Mary defended. "She's aptly named."

"Unfortunately, people aren't any different about choosing their pets than they are about choosing their partners. I'm afraid you might be stuck with that dog for a long time. Appearance matters. Note that you didn't choose to name her "Beauty" when the other volunteer pulled her from the pound and then dumped her on you at the last minute."

Mary brought her chin up. "Beauty is in the eyes of the beholder. Angel's forever family will see past her…challenges…to her sweet personality. I simply haven't had time to find them. Besides, it's not like I didn't know that I was taking on a special case when I let Rhonda Blankenship leave her with me."

"I know. I know. But I also witnessed your call to the rescue director. I heard her swear on her mother's grave that she would find a dog sitter over Christmas if you agreed to step in for Rhonda and take the new dog."

Mary shrugged. "Things happen."

"Right. And women elope and bail on commitments at the last minute all the time. So where did Rhonda and her new husband move to again?"

"Yap. It's an island in the South Pacific. It's supposed to be beautiful."

Eliza rolled her eyes and drawled, "I hope they'll be very happy. So that's it, then? You have no choice but to take that poor, pitiful, diarrhetic dog with you on a fourteen-hour car trip, then foist her off on your parents for two weeks? They're going to love that."

"They won't mind. Much. They're both dog lovers, although Mom does prefer little dogs."

"Nothing about Angel is little. She's a horse. A big, hairy horse."

"She's a big dog, yes, but don't forget she's carrying extra weight."

"I don't see how, considering that she tosses her cookies every time she eats. Oh, Mary. I'm going to worry about your road-warrioring in a seen-better-days Ford uphill through the blizzard with only a big, ugly, sick dog for company."

Mary gave her friend a chastising look. "Number one, my car might have a lot of miles, but it runs like a champ. Number two, I'm going to pretend I didn't hear the U-word. Number three, I've checked the travel conditions between Dallas and Eternity Springs, and nobody is predicting a blizzard to hit in the next two days. It's two to four inches of snow at the most once I reach the mountains, and I'll most likely be home before it starts. Number four, Angel isn't sick. The pregnancy has given her a sensitive digestive system. And finally, number five, I forbid you to spend one minute thinking about me, much less worrying. I expect you to devote all your time and attention to wringing every bit of comfort and joy from your romantic Christmas vacation with Dr. Hottie. And, to assist in that endeavor, I have a little something for you."

Mary opened one of her desk drawers and removed the small, wrapped package she'd placed there earlier.

"Mary!" Eliza exclaimed. "We already exchanged gifts. I love, love, love, love the organizer you gave me."

"I'm glad. This is a little something extra. It's my heart gift."

Eliza's eyes widened. Her voice held a note of wonder as she accepted the box, saying, "But…you didn't have time this year. You've only just finished your dad's gift. You're giving your siblings IOU's. You didn't even have time for the big fat family tradition event that's so important to you, your 'Gift of Giving to a Stranger.' But you took the time to make something for me?"

Mary could have pointed out how Eliza never failed to be there for her during the breakup with Travis. She could have talked about their excellent working relationship or the way Eliza always made her laugh when Mary really needed a laugh. But instead, she simply said, "You're my best friend, Eliza."

Her best friend burst out in uncharacteristic tears and tore into her present. "Booties! You knitted booties for me!"

"For the plane ride."

"Because I always kick my shoes off, and my feet always freeze. They're so soft. They're like a turquoise cloud. They're perfect. Thank you, Mary. I love them." Eliza threw her arms around her friend and gave her a hard hug. "There's only one problem. No way I won't think about you when I'm wearing them."

9

"Fair enough. You have permission to think about me only while you're sitting in First Class, wearing my booties, and sipping a Mai Tai."

"It's a deal. I'll drink a toast to you and Angel and tap my turquoise heels three times and wish you safely home over the river and through the woods without encountering a tornado or a blizzard or a cat named Toto."

"No cats. Angel doesn't care for cats."

Both women turned at the sound of the loading dock's buzzer. The cleanup crew had arrived. Eliza took one last sip of her champagne and set down the flute. "I've got the after-party. Consider it my heart gift to you. Stay here and wrap your presents, then go home and get a good night's sleep so that you and Angel can get an early start in the morning."

Mary accepted the gift in the spirit it was offered, and she gave her friend one more hug. "Thank you. Merry Christmas, Eliza."

"Merry Christmas, Mary." Booties in hand and whistling "I Saw Mommy Kissing Santa Claus," she left the office. A minute later, she ducked back inside and tossed something toward Mary, saying, "Since you're so big on Christmas traditions, I think you should stick this in your purse."

Jingle bells jangled as Mary caught the red ribbon holding the sprig of mistletoe that had been part of their decoration.

Eliza said, "You want to be the Girl Scout Elf when you're out walking Angel and run into Santa Hunk. Always prepared, you know."

"Santa Hunk?

"I know you are spending Christmas in a small, isolated town with a shortage of single guys, but hey, it's the season of miracles, right? Put it in your purse, Mary."

Mary laughed, did as she was told, then returned to her gift wrapping. She finished up quickly. After checking with her partner, who assured her that everything was under control, she headed home to bed.

Mary dreamed vividly that night. Snow swirled in peppermint scented air, but there were no clouds in the inky blue sky, only a full moon and a million stars. She was flying. She was flying in a sleigh pulled by reindeer—with Angel in Rudolf's lead position. Angel's nose glowed red, and around her neck hung a St. Bernard's cask of brandy. Bing Crosby crooned about a white Christmas from the sleigh's sound system speakers.

Mary wore her green Christmas party dress, a red felt hat with jingle bells and pointed tip, and sparkling Judy Garland ruby slippers with curled, pointy toes. Was the curl because they were elf shoes, or because mistletoe hung above the sleigh, and Santa Hunk had kissed her all across the Pacific?

When the sleigh sailed past an airliner headed toward Hawaii, she came up for air long enough to give Eliza a beauty queen wave. Eliza lifted her Mai Tai in a toast.

Mary awoke with a smile on her face.

As a rule, she wasn't one to put any stock in the notion that dreams foretold the future. Still, right before she backed her loaded-up eight-year-old Ford Explorer out of the driveway, she added a new song to her playlist for the trip.

Mary Landry headed home to Eternity Springs, Colorado, for Christmas, singing along to "Santa Baby."

CHAPTER 2

ANGEL MIGHT NOT BE A PRETTY PUP, BUT SHE PROVED TO BE an excellent traveling companion. Since the dog was too big for the passenger seat, Mary had placed Angel's bed on the back bench seat where she rode contentedly. Upon occasion, the dog would stand on the floorboard, stick her head between the seats, and rest it on the console. With plenty of pit stops and small snacks instead of full meals, they managed to avoid any accidents in the car, and the first day of travel passed without incident. They spent a pleasant night in a pet-friendly hotel in Amarillo and were on the road by eight a.m. the morning of the twenty-second.

Driving through New Mexico, Mary got her first glimpse of the mountains, and the sense of coming home swept over her. "Wait until you see it, Angel. Eternity Springs at Christmastime is a magical place, a Victorian village come to life. And the people who live there are all so nice. In fact, now that I think about it…"

She gave the mutt a sidelong glance. "They are dog people. True dog lovers. Why didn't I think about this before? Like Eliza said, Christmas is the season of miracles. Maybe you were meant to make the trip with me to Eternity Springs. Maybe this is where you'll find your perfect forever family."

Her spirits rising like the altitude, Mary turned up the volume of the Christmas carols she played and sang her way towards home.

She was well into the mountains, a little more than two hours from home when the trouble started. The gentle snow-fall she'd been enjoying for the past half hour intensified. The air thickened. The wind began to whip and swirl and howl. Visibility dropped to less than a car length in front of her, and Mary's nerves stretched tight.

She leaned forward, her gaze focused intently upon the winding, two-lane mountain road. Was it a good thing or a bad thing that she hadn't seen another car since turning off the main highway half an hour ago? Eternity Springs was an isolated town, to be sure, but usually, the road going that direction had more traffic.

She decided to go with "good thing." With road conditions like this, she was thankful not to worry about the skill—or lack thereof—of other drivers. Mary was a good driver, and she had new tires. Traction wasn't bad. Slow and steady would get her there in one piece. She was lucky this was a snowstorm and not ice. Mary didn't attempt to drive on ice.

As the Explorer ascended steadily toward another summit, it occurred to her that she could be traveling through a microclimate that would end over this ridge. It wasn't an outlandish idea. She had rechecked the weather forecast before leaving the hotel this morning. The two-to-four inches of snow predicted to begin falling late this afternoon had not changed. She tried calling her dad to update the weather, but she couldn't get a signal.

Unfortunately, visibility worsened rather than improved when she topped that ridge and began descending the mountain. Time and her car's progress slowed to a near crawl. Sensing the escalating tension, Angel whimpered, wedged a chunk of herself between the front seats, and plopped her large paw in Mary's lap. Giving comfort or seeking it, Mary didn't know or care. She was just glad to have the company.

"Oh ti-i-dings of co-om- fort and joy—comfort and joy..." Mary softly sang as the vehicle crept along. She didn't like driving switchbacks on clear, sunny days, much less during snowstorms. The edge of the mountain always seemed a little too close. "A-and ti-i-dings of co-om-fort and joy."

Once she finished "God Rest Ye Merry Gentlemen," she sang two more traditional carols in a squeaky tone. Finally, she reached the last curve of the switchback. Mary sang the Hallelujah Chorus, popped a peppermint breath mint, and offered Angel a biscuit from the treat box.

The snowstorm didn't abate. However, now that the road wound alongside a stream at the bottom of a mountain rather than climbing to go up and over, the journey felt less perilous. Mary relaxed and launched into "Up on the Housetop." She followed that with "Santa Claus is Coming to Town." She was on the second stanza of "Rudolf" when Angel's ears perked, her head jerked up, and—

A reindeer darted out of the woods right in front of the Ford Explorer.

CHAPTER 3

IT ALL HAPPENED IN AN INSTANT. DASHER? DANCER? IF NOT Blitzen, then about to become Splatzen. Raised in the country, Mary knew better than to swerve, but nevertheless, she reacted instinctively. She jerked her wheel to the left.

"No!" Mary barely missed clipping the antlered animal on the brisket.

He bounded off so fast he could have been flying—so maybe he really was a reindeer—and disappeared into the veil of white even as the Explorer's superior tires lost purchase.

The vehicle began an out-of-control, slow-motion slide while Angel barked and Mary gasped. The Explorer made a full circle and skidded off the road, a headlight blowing out after grazing a tree, then bumping and scraping until it thudded to a halt with both passenger-side wheels planted in a stream.

Mary released a shuddering breath. "Okay. We're okay." Up the mountain creek without a paddle or a snow shovel, perhaps, but nobody was bleeding.

They'd been lucky. A guy she'd gone to high school with

had died when he'd hit a deer and flipped his car. A friend of her father's had collided with an elk one November up near the summit of Sinner's Prayer Pass, and he'd remained in the hospital past Valentine's Day. The Explorer wasn't running and she'd lost a headlight, but the airbags hadn't deployed. Maybe the SUV was drivable. She pulled her phone from the console and checked the connection. Still no service.

"Don't panic," she told herself. Yes, this was an isolated spot, but it wasn't the Alaskan wilderness. Someone would come along. Or maybe there would be help nearby. She met the dog's big brown eyes and said, "Shoot, Angel, for all I know, we could be at the base of somebody's driveway."

Mary released her seatbelt and twisted around to peer through the windows and take stock of the situation. She couldn't see a thing through the swiftly falling snow. She would have to get out of the car and survey the surroundings, but she needed to be smart about it. How stupid would it be to survive a car wreck and die of exposure?

One thing she definitely should do was to set out the reflective triangles she carried in her emergency bag. Wouldn't it be just her luck for the one car in this section of Colorado to drive by and not see her?

She grabbed her coat, hat, and gloves from the passenger seat and pulled them on. Then, in response to Angel's whimper, Mary said, "You stay in the car, sweetheart. I'll let you out for a potty break once I figure out our situation."

Then Mary sent up a quick prayer and opened the door.

The bitter cold hit her like a fist as she took a careful step down and out of the Explorer. Her foot sank in ankle-deep snow. "Lucky it's not water," she muttered, eyeing the broken ice surrounding half her car.

Moving quickly but carefully, she stepped around to the back of the SUV and opened the rear hatch. She shuffled the pile of wrapped Christmas gifts to get to the spare tire well, where she stored her emergency kit. She'd no sooner unzipped the bag and spread it open when Angel made her move.

The dog climbed over the back seat, trampled Mary's gifts, and launched herself out of the SUV.

"Angel!" Mary grabbed for her and missed. "Angel, you stop right there!"

The dog didn't listen. Ungainly but nevertheless quick, Angel bounded toward the incline leading up to the road. Mary made a split-second decision, grabbed the roll of bright red ribbon within easy reach rather than digging for the leash, stuck the ribbon in her coat pocket, and headed after the dog. "Angel! Heel! Stop! Please, Angel. Please!"

Thankful she wore hiking boots with soles that gave her some traction, Mary climbed after the dog while a night-marish possibility flashed through her mind. If Angel dashed into the woods and disappeared, what would Mary do? Tie red ribbons around trees and go after her? In the middle of a heavy snowstorm? How foolhardy would that be? But she couldn't simply abandon the dog. "Oh, Angel. Please! Stop. Just stop!"

Mary topped the embankment. To her infinite relief, she spied a sizable brown-and-white bundle of fur standing placidly in the middle of the road. Angel glanced over her shoulder at Mary, giving her a look that said, *What took you so long?* "R-r-ruff! Ruff. Ruff. Ruff."

When Mary got within an arm's length of her, Angel took off again. "No-o-o!"

At least she stayed on the road. Mary was grateful for that. She continued to call her. She continued to scold and beg and threaten and cajole, all the while keeping her gaze locked on the dog through the curtain of falling snow.

That's why she didn't immediately notice what had Angel's attention. It was only when the dog left the road and began ascending a wooded hillside that she paused and looked up, crying out with dismay, "No, Angel, this isn't safe! "

Snow was falling harder. The wind whipped. Had the temperature dropped twenty degrees in the past ten minutes? What was she going to do? She couldn't wait. What was that a glow? Was that light? "That's a light! I see it, Angel!"

Way up the mountain shone a steady, yellow glow.

Now that she'd spied the first light, she made out three more faint ones. Windows. Those were windows in a house in the woods. A large, traditional-style log home, from the looks of it. Halfway up the mountain.

Shelter from the storm.

Relief rolled through Mary, warming her like a tropical ocean wave. Climbing up to that house would be a hike, but she had no choice but to make it. She couldn't count on another car to come along when she hadn't seen one in forever. Besides, rescuing herself was always better than waiting for rescue.

She should probably go back to the car and get her back-pack. Should she lay out the distress triangles even if she wasn't with the car? What were the rules or best practices on that?

Her stare fixed on the lights visible through the trees, Mary had momentarily lost track of the dog. As a result, she wasn't prepared when Angel's large head bumped against her leg. Mary teetered and would have fallen had she not instinc-tively grabbed hold of the dog's collar for balance.

Once she had hold of the animal, Mary wasn't letting go. She hugged Angel saying, "Thank you, Angel. You're the best puppy dog. Even if you are a misbehaving puppy dog, I'm going to cut you some slack this time. You're like the Christmas star. You led us to shelter. The place appears to be something nicer than a stable with a manger, too. A whole lot nicer."

Mary pulled the ribbon roll from her pocket, threaded the end through the ring on Angel's collar, and allowed the strand to unwind. She ended up with a three-foot leash for Angel. "Not the strongest, but better than nothing. Let's go back to the car, Angel, and get a few things before we attempt that climb."

But when she took a step back toward the car and gave the makeshift leash a tug, Angel didn't budge. "C'mon, girl. We need supplies from the car before we go for help. Treats. Let's go get puppy treats from the car."

Angel wasn't having any of it. In fact, she took off uphill, dragging Mary along with her. It quickly became clear that the ribbon leash would serve more as a guideline for Mary than a leash for the dog.

The woods were thick, the incline steep and rocky, the wind harsh, and the snowfall intense. Climbing the mountain to the beacon of light above took well over an hour. Luckily, her cold-weather gear combined with the exercise kept her from freezing her jingle bells off. As they drew closer to the house, Mary realized they were coming up to it from the backside. No wonder she had not seen a driveway.

Mary was cold, tired, and thirsty, and she hoped that whoever had the lamps lit would be kind and welcoming to a stranger in need. A stranger and her dog. Her big, pregnant, beauty-challenged foster dog.

"It will be okay," she said to Angel. "We're close to Eternity Springs. Everyone is nice in Eternity Springs. Everyone likes dogs. It'll be okay. After all, I don't think that as a rule, serial killers live in million-dollar mountain homes."

For that matter, lots of Texans owned second homes in this part of the world. It's not beyond the realm of possibility that she and Eliza had catered a party for whoever would answer the door of the large log home they were approaching.

"We're here, Angel. Finally. Thank God." Please, God. Let the owner be a Good Samaritan and not a serial killer.

Mary considered going around to the home's front door, but now that she'd arrived, exhaustion overcame her. She didn't want to take a single extra step. Not seeing a doorbell, she filled her lungs with frigid cold air, exhaled in a rush, then knocked three times on the back door.

Nothing.

She could hear music coming from inside the house. The occupants probably hadn't heard her knock. She tried again, banging harder this time. *Knock. Knock. Knock.*

Again. Nothing.

Knock knock knock. Knock knock knock.

Nothing.

Knock knock knock knock knock knock knock. "Hello? Hello!" *Knock knock knock knock knock.* "Hello? Is anyone home?"

Knock knock knock knock. At that point, Angel lost patience. Using her most resounding big-dog voice, she started barking and didn't stop.

Suddenly, while the momentum of Mary's knocking carried her forward, the door was wrenched violently open. Her legs weak as boiled noodles from the strenuous climb up the mountain, Mary lost her balance.

She wondered if she'd also lost her mind. Just how far, how high, had she climbed?

He had thick, snowy white hair that fell to his shoulders and a full beard the same color as his hair. His eyes winter-ice blue, his cheekbones chiseled. His broad shoulders tapered to a six-pack rather than a bowl full of jelly. He wore Christmas red briefs that rode low on his hips and cradled a substantial package.

Mary tumbled.

Right into Santa Hunk's arms.

CHAPTER 4

NICHOLAS CARSTAIRS MADE HIS MONEY IN MURDER. Specifically, he hosted and produced "What was he thinking?" a wildly successful True Crime podcast. The show had grown in popularity beyond his wildest imaginings and changed his life, mainly for the better. He was flush, for one thing. Seriously flush. Unless he did something stupid—and Nick wasn't stupid—he should never need to worry about money again. Not bad for a third-generation Denver cop.

Couldn't beat the working conditions with the new gig, either. Nick worked from home on his own schedule. Got to choose the cases he investigated and crawl into whatever rabbit holes he wanted to explore. He'd burrowed down a deep hole last night, digging in after his frozen entree supper and working until dawn. Indulging his night owl tendencies was the reason why he was still in bed at two o'clock in the afternoon. Having the opportunity to sleep late was the lone bright spot in this train wreck of a holiday season.

Thinking about Christmas was not how Nick wanted to begin his day, so he rolled over onto his stomach and tried to go back to sleep.

The house was quiet. Too damned quiet.

He pulled a pillow over his head. He wanted another hour or so of shut-eye, then a workout before the storm that was due to arrive around the time dark moved in. He would ski that nice little cross-country trail that took a couple hours to complete. After that, he'd put some time in on the table he was making for the kitchen. Nick liked building things. He found woodworking particularly satisfying, especially since Mikey had started showing an interest in it.

At the thought of his son, the idea of working on his table lost any appeal. Fine. He'd get a head start on January's shows. He would work ahead. That way, when Mikey came home, he'd have even more free time than usual. Maybe the two of them could take a vacation, something just as fun as Walt Disney World. Mikey liked to—

Stop it. It's not a competition. Sleep. Go to sleep.

Nick went up on his elbow, punched his pillow to fluff it, then lay back down.

Then the blasted woodpecker that had been hammering away outside his office window every day for the past week started in again. Damned bird must be what woke him to begin with. He respected and appreciated wildlife as much as the next guy, but that blasted bird had an entire forest of trees at his disposal. He needed to pick somewhere else to peck today.

Nick pulled a pillow over his head again.

The hammering continued, but along with it came a new noise. An awful sound somewhere between a howl and a screech. Sounded like an animal was caught in a trap.

Nick's brow furrowed. Had somebody been setting traps on his land? The back end of his property bordered a remote section of a national forest. Some sketchy characters roamed those woods at times. Maybe he'd better go investigate.

Bang. Bang. Bang. Bang. Bang. Howl! Nick threw off the pillow and rolled out of bed. He'd stumbled halfway toward his bedroom door when a fact sliced through his sleep-muddled brain. Those noises weren't a bird pecking at his tree or a trapped animal. Instead, someone was knocking—no, pounding—at his back door. And whoever it was had a dog with them—a loud, howling dog.

Switching directions, he headed through the kitchen to the mudroom. He opened the back door, and a woman blew in with the snow.

He caught her when she fell.

She was tiny, light as a snowflake, and pretty. Really pretty, with fiery red, shoulder-length hair, big green eyes, and a creamy complexion with cheeks rosy from the cold. She wore a red puff coat, a green knit hat, and matching gloves trimmed with white fur. She looked like an elf. She looked like Christmas.

And didn't that just ratchet his cranky up a notch? If he'd wanted Christmas in his house this year, he'd have stuck a thumbtack in a sweat sock and rammed it into the fireplace mantle. Having an enticing elf blow into his arms wasn't a welcome development. It didn't help that she was cold and wet, and he was all but bare-ass naked.

He didn't drop her, but he did set her down as quickly as possible. Indoors, which was nice of him, considering. Then he slammed the door against the wind and swirling snow. Shutting Christmas inside.

So, when his gaze fell upon her companion, all wrapped up in red ribbon, Nick's response reflected his mood. "Did I miss Halloween?"

"Excuse me?" the elf asked in a breathless tone.

"Your four-footed Frankenstein." Nick gestured at the dog.

"I'll have you know, her name is Angel."

Angel was no breed Nick recognized. She was the size of a St. Bernard, had the coat of a Newfie, a hound dog's floppy ears, and the pointed snout like a Shepard. She had one brown eye and one blue eye and a scar that crossed her forehead like laces on a football. She was one butt-ugly dog. "Not much of a looker, is she?" Nick asked.

The woman straightened her spine and squared her shoulders. Her chin came up, and her green eyes flashed. Her tone went as frosty as the snowflakes that sprinkled her from head to toe like powdered sugar. "I daresay you wouldn't be nearly so pretty if a car's grill had split your head open and you were sewn back together by a veterinary student volunteer rather than a high dollar plastic surgeon."

Nearly so pretty? Nick scowled and folded his arms. "Excuse me, have we met?"

The woman grimaced and closed her eyes. She must have loosened her hold on the behemoth because the dog pushed her way past Nick and dragged her red ribbon leash through the mudroom and into the kitchen. She plopped down beneath a heat vent and made herself at home.

"Angel, come back here!" Embarrassment added another layer of cherry to the woman's complexion. "I'm sorry. I apologize. For Angel and for the overly personal comment. It's just been a rough few hours. We are cold and exhausted, and you could be modeling underwear for GQ magazine. Yikes!" She grimaced and slapped her gloves against her hat. "I did it again. I'm so sorry."

Nick almost reached beyond her for one of the jackets that hung beside the door, but no. It wasn't long enough to cover the important parts. Besides, this was his house. If she thought he was GQ material, he'd just give her a thrill.

The elf continued babbling. "No, you and I have not met.

25

I'm Mary Landry. I live in Dallas now, but I grew up in Eternity Springs. I'm on my way home for Christmas, and the snowstorm started hours before it was forecast to begin. I hit Dasher, and my car slid into the creek, and I don't have cell service." She pulled a phone from her coat pocket to display the evidence.

Dasher? And, the elf had a Santa case for her phone? Of course, she did.

"But when I got out of the car to place the distress reflectors...hallelujah!" The woman beamed. "Angel spied your light that shined like the Christmas star leading me here. It's a really nice stable you have."

"You're mixing your Christmas metaphors," Nick grumbled.

"True. I figure it is better to mix them up than to forget the reason for the season altogether, don't you?"

Maybe hypothermia has her mind muddled. Or, she could be faking everything. Suspicious, Nick narrowed his gaze. He'd learned the hard way that a podcast focused on murders attracts some crazies. Despite being careful about his security from the beginning, he'd had more than a few "fans" show up at his door. It was one of the main reasons he'd chosen to move to this remote area of Colorado two years ago. So, was this crazy Christmas lady a murder groupie or simply a crazy Christmas lady?

"Do you have phone service here? If so, may I use your phone to call a tow truck?"

Between her guileless big green eyes and the lack of any vibration in his B.S. antennae made sensitive by six years as a detective with the Denver police department, Nick leaned more toward her being a traveler than a stalker. However, he still intended to be cautious. He nodded. "I have cell service. I'll call the tow truck for you. We only have one in the area, and the driver is a friend of mine. Come on in and warm up."

Her lips twisted with a crooked smile. "I'll make a mess. I'm dripping."

He pointed toward the mudroom closet, which had a drain inside. "Leave your wet things in there. I'll find something you can wear on your feet." Mikey's slippers should do for her, tiny as she was. "My phone is upstairs. Help yourself to coffee. Creamer is in the fridge. The bathroom is the first door on the left."

"Thank you so much."

The relief that washed across her face caused Nick a twinge of guilt. But only a twinge. Even if she proved to be a stranded traveler instead of a lunatic groupie, the woman *had* brought Christmas into his house. Christmas was the absolute last thing he wanted or needed.

Up in his bedroom, Nick dressed in jeans and a sweatshirt, then grabbed his phone, shoved his feet into his slippers, and headed for his son's room. He dug through the boy's closet, looking for the birthday gift the kid had received from Nick's great aunt. Unfortunately, the two sizes too big moccasins weren't there. Nick looked under the bed, searched the dresser drawers, and finally found them in the playroom where Mikey was using them as a parking garage for his Hot Wheels cars.

Nick headed for the stairs with the prize in one hand, thumbing through his phone contacts for Pete Wilson's number with the other. As the call connected and began to ring, he heard a sound coming from his kitchen that made his eyes widen in surprise—the whir of coffee beans in the grinder. She was making real coffee? Not the single-serve pod stuff that Nick made himself every day?

He had all the supplies and paraphernalia because his ex

27

had been a coffee snob, and he kept it for when he had guests. He'd lived on precinct coffee for years, so he could drink paint thinner, but he did enjoy a superior cup of joe. So, if Mary Christmas had made a pot for sharing, he guessed it wouldn't hurt to suspend his Grinch and tolerate an hour of holiday with an elf.

Distracted by the aroma of freshly ground beans, Nick took a moment to respond when Pete answered his call. He explained the situation, and Pete promised to head his way as soon as he finished working on his current service call. Unfortunately, he was twenty minutes north of Eternity Springs, which put him probably two hours away from Nick. Okay, two pots of good coffee.

"I'll give you a shout when I'm getting close," Pete said.

"Thanks, Pete," Nick disconnected the call and descended the stairs. He almost tripped on the last step when his uninvited guest turned around, and he got his first good look at her sans coat and scarf and hat and gloves.

Whoa, she packed a punch. Not just pretty, but beautiful. No bigger than a minute and more curves than the road up Sinner's Prayer Pass. Sexy as sin. He had an immediate, visceral response to her, which was about as welcome as Christmas.

This latest skirmish with Lauren about the holidays had churned up all the ugly memories surrounding their breakup and put him off women like a bad sushi supper. This physical reaction to his uninvited guest resurrected his Grinch, so he spoke gruffly as he handed her his son's slippers. "See if these will do. If not, I'll get you some socks."

"Thank you. My feet are freezing."

"You're welcome." He watched as she slipped her pint-sized toes into Mikey's shoes. Bright red nail polish. Of course. What else would an elf wear? Nick forced his gaze away from her feet, but then it snagged on her chest.

Her sweater was white with a green felt triangle Christmas tree and a string of multicolored pompoms for lights. Pompoms all over her pompoms. A star made of gold glitter topped the tree, and the felt boxes at its base were wrapped with actual ribbon. It was a three-dimensional disaster. "That sweater is…."

"Terrible, isn't it?" The crazy lady lit up like an outdoor light display and preened. "You wouldn't believe how hard I had to shop to find a Christmas sweater this ugly. They've become way too popular. Wearing one for homecoming is a family tradition. Even though we're all about handmade Christmas gifts, it's against our rules to make our ugly sweaters. They have to be store-bought."

"Homecoming? Do y'all have a dance, too? Next, you'll be throwing in the Thanksgiving turkey."

She laughed, an appealing sparkle of a sound, and poured a cup of coffee, which she'd made with the French press. "I made enough for two. Do you want-"

"Yes."

He picked up the mug and savored the aroma before taking a sip. Whoa. Mary Christmas's coffee was better than his ex's. Better than what they served at the Mocha Moose in Eternity Springs. Definitely a Grinch-crusher. Nick could have kissed her. When his gaze drifted to her full lips as she sipped and savored her own coffee, he realized he *wanted* to kiss her.

Dammit, Carstairs. What's wrong with you?

She'd addled his brain, that's what. All that sparkle she was throwing around probably had some elf woo-woo dust in it.

Or maybe you've been alone too long.

"Coffee's good." He turned away and prowled over to the fireplace where he set about making a fire. "Tow truck is north of Eternity Springs working another job. He said he'd be here in a couple of hours. Maybe three."

Dismay dampened her tone. "That long? Oh, dear. Angel and I are a real imposition to you. Please, don't bother with us. Return to whatever you were doing when we arrived. We will sit here and enjoy the heat and stay out your hair."

"Sleeping. I was sleeping." In his bed. Alone.

Whoosh. Nick lit the gas jets beneath the stacked wood, and the flames ignited.

"Naps on a snowy day are a wondrous thing," observed his guest.

"I worked late last night. All night."

Now she winced. "Oh, no. Not napping. You were sleeping. Now I really feel bad."

"Don't worry about it." He meant it. He needed the conversation to shift away from beds.

"Let me do something," she continued. "I make my living as a professional chef. So, if you'll allow me to scrounge around a little more in your kitchen, I'd be happy to make you something to eat."

A chef? If her food was anything like her coffee, he could tolerate two hours of Christmas. He'd been eating from a can since Mikey left, and that was getting old. "Works for me."

"Would you prefer breakfast or lunch?"

"Breakfast," he replied without hesitation. "Make yourself at home. My phone is on the mantle. You're welcome to use it to call your family. In the meantime, I'll go grab a shower." One that's a little colder than he'd typically take on a snowy winter day. He figured it might take icy cold water to wash off the sexy elf dust.

"Great. Thank you. I'll get cracking. Can I assume that

since any food I find is in your home, it's something you enjoy eating?"

Nick filled his mug with a second cup of coffee and mentally inventoried his stores.

"The Cocoa Puffs aren't mine."

"I'll make a point not to utilize Cocoa Puffs in my recipe."

He was halfway across the room headed for the stairs when she called out. "One more thing?"

He glanced over his shoulder. "Yeah?"

"What's your name? You never told me."

"Oh. I'm Nick. Nick Carstairs."

"Nick Carstairs," she repeated. Then again, more softly. "Nick Carstairs."

He was climbing the staircase when he heard her gasp and set her mug down on the counter hard. "Nicholas Carstairs. I knew I recognized your voice. I just couldn't place it."

Damn.

"It *is* you." She slapped a hand over her pompoms. "The silver hair. The true-crime podcast. 'What Was He Thinking?' That's you, isn't it?"

Nick hesitated. Just in case this was the moment when crazy Christmas lady morphed into crazy murder groupie, perhaps he should deny it. Except, he didn't peg her as a groupie. To be honest, he found it a little flattering that she was a fan.

In a horrified, accusing tone, she added, "You're the Santa Claus Killer!"

Ah, hah. Nick's uninvited guest had listened to his rather epic rant on the podcast that had dropped yesterday. One corner of his mouth lifted with a smirk. He'd been wearing his Grinch loud and proud when he'd recorded that episode, so he could see how Mary Christmas would disapprove. "You're not going to spit into my scrambled eggs now, are you?"

She wrinkled her little elfin nose. "No, but I might sprinkle them with Christmas cheer."

Nick laughed and continued up the stairs. "Don't waste your sprinkles, candy cane. I'm a Christmas lost cause. "

Nick's hearing was acute. Otherwise, he wouldn't have heard her soft murmur. "Bless his heart."

CHAPTER 5

*O*F ALL THE ISOLATED CABINS, IN ALL THE MOUNTAIN TOWNS, IN *all the world, I stumble into the Santa Claus Killer's.*

Mary's thoughts spun as she searched his pantry and refrigerator and decided on a possible menu. How crazy was this? She enjoyed listening to podcasts while she worked, and she had an eclectic playlist. Although "What Was He Thinking?" wasn't on her schedule of regulars, she had tuned in to the true-crime podcast many times. She'd have recognized him right off had she not been so flustered when she stumbled and fell into his arms.

Well, and if she hadn't been distracted by all that skin.

She liked his show. Nick Carstairs had a quick mind and a witty tongue, and he presented the cases the show explored in an intelligent, entertaining manner. In addition, she found his interviews with expert guests fascinating. He asked probing questions that made his guests think and sometimes stumped them. Mary thought that criminals had caught a break when Detective Nick Carstairs left law enforcement.

She'd had no idea he lived in Colorado, much less this close to her hometown. She didn't recall him talking about his personal life in any of his previous shows. Not that he'd revealed very much about himself yesterday during his riff on Christmas, other than his monumentally bad attitude where the holiday was concerned. When his guest, his former partner at the Denver police department, called him a Grinch, Nick rejected the name but embraced the idea. He'd declared he needed a moniker that suited his show, and the two men bandied about possibilities for a few minutes. The partner brought up Nick's distinctive hair coloring, goaded him about going gray in his twenties, and then relayed a story about a suspect who'd referred to Nick as Santa Claus. That informational tidbit took the conversation down the road that led to the birth of the Santa Claus Killer.

Mary had been appalled. She was still appalled. She was also curious, so she called her mother. After explaining the delay in general, you-need-not-worry terms, Mary asked her mother if she knew Mary's host. She'd never met him in person, but their mutual friend, Celeste Blessing, had nothing but nice things to say about him.

After promising to call with updates, Mary ended the call and returned Nick's phone to the mantle. Next, she retrieved her own phone with its downloaded music from her coat. She hummed along to "Jingle Bells" while browning the sausage in a cast-iron skillet. Soon she had onion, potatoes, and jalapeño peppers sizzling in a second pan.

With breakfast cooking, she took a moment to study her surroundings. Nick Carstairs lived in a beautiful home perched high on this mountain. She'd bet the wall of north-facing windows offered a gorgeous view on a clear day. Right now, all one could see was snow. A stone fireplace dominated another wall in the open concept great room, its mantle a vast, rough-hewn beam upon which sat a trio of intriguing modernistic metal sculptures.

Mary didn't see stockings hanging from the mantle or any other sign of the pending holiday.

Here it was only a few days before Christmas, and his home had no tree, no wreath, no poinsettias. And didn't that staircase banister cry out for garland? She spied no packages or wrapping paper or ribbon and bows. Why, he didn't even have any Christmas cards lying around, much less on display. Santa Claus Killer, indeed. The man lived up to the name. It was sad.

She wondered what had made him so anti-holiday.

Mary stirred the vegetables with a wooden spoon. Mouth-watering aromas rose and swirled in the air. His kitchen had a well-stocked spice drawer, and she made good use of it. She was hungry. Breakfast burritos would hit the spot.

As she cracked eggs into a bowl a few minutes later, Nick's footsteps sounded on the stairs. She glanced up from the eggs, and her heart gave a little patty-pat. My oh my. The man rocked his unusual coloring. He'd trimmed his beard and pulled his hair back into a queue. Instead of the sweatshirt, he wore a blue plaid flannel shirt that accentuated the blue in his eyes. Sexy voice aside, Mary couldn't help but think his looks were wasted by doing a podcast instead of film.

Daresay, the Nick Carstairs who'd answered the door in his underwear could be a star of all manner of films— including explicit ones. Mary could see the video cover now. Nick Carstairs stars in "Santa Hunk and the Vixen."

"Whatever's cooking smells delicious," he said.

Mary wrestled her wayward thoughts back to the menu at hand. "Breakfast burritos."

"Excellent. One of my favorites."

"I figured as much based on the quantity of salsa in your pantry."

Nick filled another mug with coffee. "I like heat."

"That's why you live on top of a mountain, I guess?"

"Actually, I moved up here to get away from drop-in visitors."

In the process of stirring the peppers and onions, Mary fumbled the spoon. "Ouch. Bullseye, Mr. Carstairs."

"Sorry." Grimacing, he rubbed the back of his neck. "I didn't mean that the way it sounded. I was talking about crime stalkers, not stranded travelers."

"Well this stranded traveler appreciates your hospitality. If I didn't know better, I'd assume you were acting out of Christmas spirt." She poured the beaten eggs into the skillet to cook. "So what about Santa? Did you bury him in your backyard?"

"The attic above the garage. He's in about a dozen red and green boxes. Technically, my backyard is a national forest."

"Nice. So, you haven't always been Detective Grinch if you have twelve boxes of decorations."

"It's a relatively recent development."

"So, what did the big jolly guy do to tick you off? Did he put coal in your stocking last Christmas? Or was all of that back and forth with the other detective on your show just entertainment?"

"Are all elves terriers, Mary Christmas?"

"Excuse me?"

He shook his head. "Never mind. I was playing off Dan when we recorded that episode. Maybe I exaggerated a bit, but I stand by most of what I said. Christmas today is too commercialized, too secular, too fake. It's snow in a can, artificial trees, and perfectly color-coordinated outfits for the perfect photo for the perfect family holiday card. I'm over it."

Mary wondered if he heard the bitter note in his own voice. There's a story there, she thought. "I agree that Christmas is too commercialized, and that some holiday customs have gotten out of hand. For instance, as much as I love Christmas music, I don't want to listen to it before Halloween."

"Hallelujah."

"However, it is possible to celebrate Christmas authentically." Mary judged the eggs to be done and dished them into a bowl she had set out for the purpose and continued speaking while assembling the burritos. "My family began a few special Christmas traditions specifically for that reason."

She told him about the Landry's homemade presents and their annual outreach to a stranger tradition. "We each share our gift of giving over brunch Christmas morning, and the family votes on whose gift was best. The winner is excused from kitchen duty for the rest of the day."

"That's nice," Nick said, watching her plate his meal with a hungry gaze. "Unusual."

"It was my brother's idea. We were in high school, and Jason was trying to impress a girl."

"Did it work?"

"Something worked. She and Jason married the weekend following college graduation. So in a way, Christmas helped bring them together."

"Funny how that can happen," he said as his cell phone rang. He glanced at the screen. "It's the guy with a tow truck."

Mary carried the plates to the table while Nick answered the phone. "Hey, Pete. You're earlier than I expected."

Following a long pause, he said, "I see. I haven't been watching. Okay, then. It is what it is." Another break, then, "Yeah. Sounds good. Appreciate it, man."

Mary had gone still, sensing what was coming. Nick disconnected the call and met her gaze. "Weather conditions have deteriorated rapidly. The road is closed. We're officially in blizzard territory, and the storm is forecast to continue for some time. Looks like you and Frankenstein are going to be my houseguests."

"Angel." She corrected him softly, as distracted, her thoughts began to swirl like the blowing snow outside. How long was 'some time?' Christmas Eve was the day after tomorrow. She didn't have time for a blizzard. She still had baking to do! What if the snow didn't stop? What if the road didn't open tomorrow? What if—

Stop it. Mary should count her lucky stars. She could be sitting in a wrecked car, freezing to death if not for her guardian Angel and the Santa Claus Killer. "I'm so sorry to impose on you this way."

"Don't worry about it." Nick took a bite of the fried potatoes, then murmured an appreciative, "Mm."

Next, he tasted his burrito, then closed his eyes and reverently savored. After swallowing, he met Mary's gaze with blue eyes that glowed with interest. "So, Mary Christmas, what's for supper?"

CHAPTER 6

Nick insisted on cleaning up after the meal. When he dangled a hot shower before her as an incentive, Mary didn't protest. Angel waddled beside Mary as Nick showed her to a spacious guest suite and invited her once again to make herself at home. "There's a bathrobe in the closet, and a basket of toiletries in the linen cabinet. I'll see if I can't round up a change of clothes that won't swallow you if you'd like to run your things through the washer. I'll scrounge up a bed of some sort for the dog, too. If she needs to go out, use the mudroom door. There's the spot right outside that's protected from the wind, so Frank will be able to do her business without getting lost in a snowdrift."

"Angel. Perfect. Thanks. This is a beautiful room, and a hot shower sounds perfect right now. Maybe a nap, too."

"I'll leave stuff in front of the door. Sleep well, Jingle Bell. Just holler if you need anything."

"I will. Thank you." She waited for a beat for emphasis and added, "From the bottom of my heart, thank you."

Mary was delighted with the room, but the bathroom made her want to giggle like a schoolgirl. A free-standing

39

soaking tub sat between a fireplace equipped with gas logs and a large picture window, cleverly placed to ensure privacy while at the same time offering what she bet was a ten-million-dollar view on a clear day.

Forget the shower. Mary would take a nice long hot bath in front of the fireplace, listen to music, and watch the snowfall.

When she spied the basket of paperback books next to the toiletries basket, her delight escalated. She chose a cozy mystery from the mixed-genre offering, filled the tub, and engaged the spa jets and heater. Angel turned three circles and plopped down on a rug in front of one of the vanities. "Poor baby," Mary crooned to the dog as she peeled off her clothes. "I'll bet you're exhausted."

Then, with Nick Carstairs's sexy voice echoing through her brain, she added, "Sleep well, jingle bell."

Mary moaned with pleasure as she settled into the tub for a period of bliss. For the first time in days, in weeks...no, actually in the past two months, Mary relaxed. By page eight, she'd dropped off to sleep.

She awoke forty minutes later, a little wrinkled but renewed. Angel never stirred as Mary dried off and donned the robe she found hanging in a closet. When she checked outside the bedroom door, she found the stack that Nick had promised. The bed for Angel was a soft, fluffy sleeping bag. The change of clothes he'd offered Mary had her wrinkling her brow in doubt until she saw the possibilities. She'd look like a fool, but it'd be nice to have her jeans dry.

Ten minutes later, she eyed herself in the mirror. She wore a long-sleeved green wool blend men's shirt that hit her mid-thigh like a tunic. She'd belted it at the waist with a red necktie that she'd tied in a bow. The red leggings she wore beneath it were a pair of men's bike pants, rolled up at the ankles and secured with four of the safety pins Nick had included. Over the red Lycra pants, she wore thick wool socks that matched the color of the shirt. He'd cut the foot and heel out of the socks so that they could serve as leg warmers. Paired with the slippers he'd given her earlier, she looked downright festive.

The coincidence was too much. For a man who wanted nothing to do with Christmas, Nick appeared to have kept the holiday in mind as he'd made his color selections. Maybe once she put together the Irish stew that he'd requested, she'd bake a batch of sugar cookies and decorate them. Then, she could leave a little Christmas behind with him when she continued her trip to Eternity Springs. His mood had obviously improved with a good cup of coffee and breakfast in his stomach. Maybe he just needed a taste of the season to get him to a happy holiday mode.

The thought made Mary happy, so she left the guest room and went in search of her host with a spring in her step. Based on an empty mug and a yellow legal pad containing handwritten notes, he'd obviously spent some time on the sofa in front of the great room fireplace. Now the fire was banked and the room empty. However, the pulse of hard rock drifting up from a descending staircase suggested where she might find Nick Carstairs.

Mary hesitated. She had no reason to disturb him. He'd given her carte blanch in his kitchen. She should get started on supper and leave him be.

That's precisely what she did until Angel abandoned her spot in front of the fire and ambled toward the staircase. "Do you need to go out?" Mary called, thinking it was probably about that time. "Angel? Don't go down there. Leave him alone."

The dog ignored her and disappeared down into the basement. Mary sighed heavily, washed carrot peel from her hands, picked up the dishtowel, and hurried after Angel. Just as she reached the top of the stairs, the music abruptly cut off.

Uh-oh. I hope you didn't do something you shouldn't, Angel. Mary picked up her pace.

The staircase opened up to a large room with felt-paneled walls and sound equipment, which she was sure must be the studio for Nick's podcast. Interesting. She'd take a better look at it when she wasn't chasing down a hallway after her foster dog. The first walled-off room in the basement on her right was a well-equipped home gym. The second was a bathroom. Angel disappeared into a third.

As Mary approached the open doorway, she heard Nick Carstairs say in the sweetest, most gentle voice, "I love you, too."

Mary halted in her tracks.

"What did you do today, buddy? Did you go see the mouse?"

Buddy. Mouse. Not a girlfriend, then.

It was wrong to eavesdrop, Mary knew. But, wow, when was the last time she'd heard a male voice swell with so much love? It brought tears to her eyes, and she blinked them away.

"That sounds like fun. What was your favorite ride?"

Mary stepped silently toward the open door. She should be a responsible dog owner—well, dog foster mom—and make sure Angel wasn't a pest, right?

You just want to snoop.

"Wow, Mikey. That sounds really cool."

Was Mikey his son? Mary wondered. She listened intently during the long silence that followed.

Eventually, Nick cleared his throat. "You want me to call you Michael? Well, sure, you *are* growing up. If the nickname bothers you, then, of course, I'll change. Fair warning,

42

though. I'm sure to slip up from time to time. I've been calling you Mikey for almost eight years. I'll do my best, but I hope you'll cut me a little slack."

Had to be his son, a boy who was almost eight years old.

"Ah. I see. Makes more sense now. Look, I'll talk to your mom about it, okay? Don't worry. Just concentrate on having a great time with her today. You're gonna love Animal Kingdom. That's right up your alley."

Mary put the pieces together. *The boy is at Disney with his mother.*

"I'm honestly not sure, buddy. I've never been to Disney World. Although I have the impression that it has African animals like in "The Lion King." I could be wrong. Tell you what. If you don't see any bison on this trip, you and I will go back to Yellowstone this summer."

Following a moment's silence, Nick laughed softly. The sound drew Mary closer to the open door.

"I'm so glad you're having a good time with your mom, big guy. See? I told you it would all work out. I was right when I said you shouldn't worry, that your mom would take good care of you, wasn't I? She promised she'd more than make it up to you for letting you down last year."

Mary whispered, "Ah hah." Now the Christmas Killer's anti-holiday rant made more sense. Nick Carstairs must be a divorced dad separated from his child this Christmas by custody arrangements.

Her reluctant host continued. "Me? Well, nothing much is new here. No, I decided not to go. I'll wait and make that trip when you and I can go together."

Mary moved to where she could see into the room, a well-equipped home gym. Wearing a sweat-stained gray t-shirt and navy gym shorts, Nick sat on a weight bench with his back to her. He had his cell phone up to his right ear.

Angel had nuzzled up against him, and his left hand stroked her coat.

Angel, doing the comfort work.

After listening to something the boy was saying for a few moments, Nick's spine stiffened. "Your mother said that? Now, I'm gonna have to draw the line right there. Don't be afraid to ask me anything, Michael. Ever."

During the long silence that followed, Nick seemed to melt in upon himself. His voice sounded strained as he asked, "Well, buddy, what do you believe?"

Believe about what?

Nick raked his fingers through his thick silver hair. "All right, then. Don't listen to that kid. If he doesn't want to believe in Santa, that's his problem. Maybe he's been naughty instead of nice, and he's making excuses already about the coal he's expecting Santa to leave him Christmas morning. He's missing out on the magic, Mikey, and I will tell you this. I believe in Christmas magic. People talk about the spirit of Christmas. Well, I'll believe in that magic until the day I die. I've seen it up close and personal."

Oh, no. The Santa Claus question! Over the phone? Poor Nick. Poor Mikey.

"Seriously. Christmas is all about magic. Rudolph and his red nose are magic. Christmas carols are magic. The sight of the little baby Jesus in the manger at last week's Christmas pageant is magic. Yeah, yeah, yeah, I know that wasn't the real baby Jesus. That was Brick Callahan's baby girl. But that pageant was magical, and you were the best camel that Eternity Springs has ever seen! And let's not forget about James, either."

James? Who is James?

"Talk about Christmas magic. The way he keeps you in line all of December is absolutely Christmas magic.

Speaking of that crafty little elf, where did you find him this morning?"

Ah, James must be the name Nick's son chose for his Elf on the Shelf.

"Maybe he's tired from following you all over the park. But, then again, sometimes hiding in plain sight is the best hiding place of all."

Following a moment's pause, Nick gave a little laugh. "I don't know. When you come home, we will have to look. We will talk about this some more, too. Tell you what. We can both make a list of all the Christmas magic we believe in and talk about them together. Like that idea? Is that a deal? Good. Oh, and remind me to tell you my story about Frankenstein and the friendly elf."

A smile fluttered on Mary's lips.

"It's Christmas magic with a little Halloween thrown in," Nick continued. "It's too long to go into over the telephone, but you'll want to hear it. Now, I can hear your mother in the background calling you, so we'd better say goodbye. We'll talk tomorrow, okay, buddy? You have fun and don't ask any of those Disney princesses for their phone numbers. You're too young to date."

Nick lifted his face toward the ceiling, and from her angle, Mary could see the anguish reflected there. He lay back, his eyes closed, his throat tight as he said, "I love you, too, Mikey. I miss you to the moon and back, too. Yes, Merry Christmas. Talk to you tomorrow. Goodbye."

He lowered the phone and let it drop to the floor, then flung his forearm over his eyes. Angel, the little mother that she was, whimpered, nuzzled his neck, licked his cheek, then rested her head on his chest. Nick idly scratched her behind her ears.

Canine comfort and kisses for a wounded Grinch.

Christmas magic, indeed. Mary was beginning to believe that the animal in the forest had been a reindeer, after all.

Maybe the bowl-full-of-jelly belly Santa was working some of his Christmas magic for Santa Six-pack. Maybe Mary had been guided here for a purpose.

After all, didn't she still need to fulfill her family's traditional gift of giving to a stranger? She needed to check that box so she would have something to share with her family on Christmas morning. She could give Nick something to make him feel less lonely and miserable. She could show the Santa Claus Killer the error of his ways.

Mary backed away from the gym, turned, and headed quietly up the stairs. She had Irish stew to put on and a gift of giving to prepare—something right up her alley.

From now until the tow truck arrived, Mary Landry was going to remind Nick Carstairs of the healing magic of Christmas by giving him the gift of Christmas cheer.

Even if it killed them both.

CHAPTER 7

When Nick awoke the following morning, memories of the previous evening rolled over him, leaving him vaguely ashamed. He owed the sexy little elf an apology. He'd been an absolute ass after Mikey's call.

Nick had hidden in the basement until savory aromas and the sound of Mary calling his name lured him upstairs. She'd served him the best Irish stew he'd eaten in his life, and he'd said little more than a gruff thank you before ushering her off to the theater room to watch a movie. She'd wanted to watch a Christmas flick, of course. So, he'd put on "Die Hard" then sneaked out of the room and slithered back downstairs to hide and imbibe. Nick wasn't much of a drinker as a rule, but last night he'd polished off half a bottle of scotch.

He missed his son like a limb. While his ex might be showing all the proper maternal instincts and attributes right now, he knew better than to trust that Lauren would keep her poop in a group for long. She would fall off the wagon and disappear from Mikey's life, leaving Nick to pick up the pieces. Again. As was her pattern. Been there, done this, got the divorce because of it.

No, she'd be around just long enough to screw up Christmas by putting Michael in the orbit of someone who just has to spill the beans about Santa Claus while standing in line at Disney World. Wonderful. Just effing wonderful.

Still, all that was no excuse to be a jerk to Mary. Nick rolled out of bed and headed for a long, hot shower and a pair of aspirin while framing the apology he intended to make. He was halfway to the master bathroom when the scene outside his bedroom window finally permeated his thoughts.

Whoa. So much for waking to a blue, sunny sky this morning. The wind was blowing like a banshee with near-zero visibility. So much for yesterday's forecast. The blizzard wasn't done yet. Judging by the height of the snowbanks in Nick's front yard, he bet at least a couple of feet of the fluffy stuff had fallen since Mary Landry knocked on his front door.

As he stepped naked beneath the steaming shower a few minutes later, Nick accepted the fact that the day's plans had changed. Even if it stopped snowing by the time he dried off, Pete would not be able to get up here with a tow truck today. The snowplows would need to do their thing first, and as always, it would take some time for them to scrape their way to Nick's little piece of paradise. Mary Christmas and her mutt were here for another day.

Nick was shocked to realize that he didn't really mind the company.

As a result, he had a spring in his step as he headed downstairs that got a little perkier when he caught a whiff of bacon, and…was that gingerbread?

Whoa, mama. He loved gingerbread.

The pantry door stood open, and noises seeped out from inside. Nick detoured toward the coffee pot, poured himself a mug, then wandered to the pantry. "What the hell?"

The elf was on his shelf.

The step stool was open and placed in front of the shelves on the pantry's back wall. Mary sat perched on a shelf perpendicular to the back wall, a good six feet off the ground. In the process of reaching for a box on the uppermost shelf, she glanced down at him and smiled. "Good morning."

"What are you doing? You're gonna break your neck."

"You have a pasta press attachment for your mixer. I'm going to use it for the marzipan."

"I have marzipan?"

"You will when I'm done. You have all the basic ingredients." Her fingertips brushed a box on the top shelf, but she couldn't get a good grip. "We're going to make a gingerbread house."

We? "You and Frank?"

"You and me."

"Not in this…would you be careful, please? You're gonna give me a heart attack. Here." He set down his coffee, stepped up on the stool, and grabbed the mixer attachment box. After setting it on a low shelf, he lifted his hands toward her. "Come down. Carefully. Please."

She shrugged and scooted toward him. Nick grasped her waist, eased her off the shelf, and held her, planning for a slow, controlled descent. It took longer than intended because, well, the pantry was smaller than he'd remembered. The air inside it was suddenly thicker.

He hadn't held a woman by the waist in longer than he could recall.

A tiny waist at that. Nick's hands all but spanned it. "You really are no bigger than a minute," he murmured, staring into her luminous green eyes. "An elf on my shelf."

With lips as red as a bowl full of cherries. Nick needed more fruit in his diet. A man had to stay healthy, after all. He brought her closer, his gaze fastened on her mouth, telegraphing his intention. She licked her lips. He moved in for the kiss.

A force hit the back of his knees, knocking him forward. He shifted so as not to crush her against the shelves and banged his funny bone in the process. He damned near dropped his elf.

"Arf. Arf. Arf."

"Frankenstein!" Nick snapped.

"Angel," Mary corrected, swooping up the mixer attachment and slipping past him.

Nick muttered a curse, retrieved his mug of coffee, and exited the pantry rubbing his aching funny bone and trying to gather his thoughts. What the heck had just happened?

The elf woo-woo dust again, he surmised. Mary must emit the stuff like pheromones.

While she busied herself doing something with his mixer, Nick studied her. This morning she wore her pompom sweater and jeans again, but she'd added his makeshift leg warmers to the look. He found himself wondering if she'd worn them to bed. "Did you sleep all right last night?"

"I did. Your guest room is like the Ritz. The bed is a toasty, comfy cloud of luxury. I didn't want to leave it. I might still be cuddled up in it reading had Angel not needed to go out. Don't even get me started about the sumptuous bathroom."

"So, if you let the dog out, then you know that the blizzard's still blowing."

"Yes, that was hard to miss."

"Well, the problem is that we've had so much snow that Pete will need the plows to get out before he'll be able to make it up here with his tow truck. I have my doubts that'll happen today."

Mary nodded. "Yes, I figured as much. Looks like you'll

be stuck with houseguests for another day. I would say that I'm sorry to impose on you, but the thing is, I'm not sorry. "

"You like my bed that much?" he asked before he could stop himself. He really needed to drag his mind back out of the elf dust. He absolutely wouldn't verbalize his next thought. *I could join you there and make it even more inviting.*

Mary Christmas lit up with a twinkling smile. "Ooh, I didn't think that far ahead. I get another night in paradise."

Just say the word, sugar cookie.

"But first, we have a busy day ahead of us. I figured it all out last night. You see, I believe in the magic of Christmas. I believe in reindeer games. And I believe I'm meant to spend this time with you, Nicholas. I'm here to help you put your money where your mouth is."

"What are you talking about?"

"I'm gonna be candid and open with you. While I was attempting to keep Angel corralled last night, I heard you talking to your son."

Nick's spine stiffened. He folded his arms over his broad chest. "You eavesdropped on my private and personal conversation? Seriously?"

"I did."

"Have you no manners? I ought to kick you out into the cold."

She wasn't one bit flustered. "It wasn't intentional. Not at first, anyway. I caught Angel going somewhere she didn't belong, and I went to retrieve her. I know that eavesdropping is a violation of your privacy, and ordinarily, I would apologize for my bad manners. However, in this situation, I can't apologize because I'm not sorry I did it. I believe it was meant to be because I believe."

Nick waited for her to finish her sentence. And when she didn't, he asked, "Believe in what?"

"In Christmas, of course. Now, tell me about your son. From what I overheard, he's seven years old and spending Christmas at Disney World with his mother? When is he coming home? You know, there is absolutely no reason why Mikey can't have a second Christmas morning with his dad— even if the date of it is January."

Nick set down his coffee mug and folded his arms. "You have more nerve than a toothache."

"I'm passionate. I have conviction. I believe the elk that made me swerve off the road might well have been a reindeer after all. I believe that Angel was supposed to be with me in my Explorer yesterday. And that she was meant to follow the star to your luxurious stable and find her way to the basement at the exact time you needed a pup to pet. And I believe I never found time to give a gift to a stranger because you are the stranger I'm supposed to gift."

"You're nervy *and* crazy."

She flashed him a happy-hearted smile. "Maybe. But I am definitely filled with the Spirit of Christmas. What you see here is the magic of the holiday season at work. You believe in Christmas magic. I heard you say so to your son."

"He was asking the Santa Claus question. Two days before Christmas, when he's two thousand miles away from me. What was I supposed to say?"

"I think you did a great job with your response. I also think you spoke the truth. You do believe in the magic of Christmas. You've just locked it up and buried it this year. Luckily, Angel and I came equipped with a shovel and a church-key. While we're waiting for this storm to blow over, we are going to decorate your home. I'm going to give you the gift of Christmas cheer."

"Thanks, but no thanks. I'm just fine with my status quo as a Grinch."

"Unacceptable, sir. The Grinch has got to go." The kitchen timer dinged, and Mary grabbed a hot pad and sauntered to the oven. Then, glancing over her shoulder, she gave Nick a spritely wink and declared, "It's time for the Santa Claus Killer to get his Christmas on."

CHAPTER 8

B<small>Y</small> <small>MID-AFTERNOON</small>, M<small>ARY</small> <small>DECIDED</small> <small>THAT</small> <small>SHE'D</small> <small>NEVER</small>
worked so hard in her life. The man was stubborn. Killing the
Santa Claus Killer might well be the end of her.

She'd pushed and prodded and badgered him into
grudging cooperation. Then, finally, he bought into the idea
that having a second Christmas morning with his son could
help him successfully navigate the Santa Claus waters. Still,
he resisted the cheer she was trying so hard to give him.

They negotiated the activities she had planned for the day
throughout the gingerbread house assembly. That task took
twice as long as usual because the man kept "accidentally"
demolishing walls and eating the broken pieces. Nick
Carstairs had quite the sweet tooth.

He resisted making a trip to the attic to unearth the
Christmas decorations he'd buried there. However, the day
was saved when Mary discovered the hot glue gun Nick and
his son used for scout projects. A determined woman could
do a lot of decorating while armed with a hot glue gun.

With Christmas music playing over the sound system,
Mary got crafty. First, she braved the blizzard to harvest the

pinecones, sticks, and bits of evergreen that had blown up against the house. Next, she popped popcorn and raided Nick's desk for paper and pens and scissors and string. She gathered art supplies from Mikey's playroom and requisitioned pasta from the pantry. Then, having transformed the dining table into a workstation and assigned tasks to Nick, Mary got to work creating a wreath, garland, and ornaments for the tree. Her host had reluctantly agreed to harvest a blue spruce from his property as soon as the storm abated. For that concession, she mixed up a batch of sugar cookies.

She finally managed to find a crack in his bah-humbug attitude when she started folding paper stars for the tree. Nick proved to be an origami expert. The paper-folding process served to relax him. He made a darling paper dog, and that led the conversation around to pets. She told him about her work with Wags and Walks Rescue and how she came to be traveling the road to Eternity Springs with Angel.

He deflected most of her questions about his son and displayed his detective skills with subtle questions about her life. She found herself talking about Travis. "You call me an elf. Well, I'm absolutely an elf on the shelf." She told Nick about the breakup, and he responded with all the ego-stroking things that a girl liked to hear. Mary could have kissed him.

She *wanted* to kiss him.

She had wanted to dump the contents of the flour canister on Angel's head when the dog interrupted the almost-kiss moment in the pantry. Too bad her haul of pinecones and evergreens hadn't included any mistletoe. Maybe when they went out to harvest a tree, she could solve that little problem. If not, as a last resort, she did have that fake mistletoe bough in her purse from the Landry and Lawrence Catering Christmas party. Nick wouldn't like it any better than canned snow, but he would need to make do.

Because she needed his kiss.

Mary's gaze drifted toward the wall of windows, and she realized that for the first time since shortly after her arrival yesterday, she could see something other than snow. "Look, Nick. The sky is clearing."

"Finally. It's nice to see the sun."

"It's beautiful," she murmured in reply. "It's all beautiful. The way the sunlight sparkles on the snow makes it look like your front yard is filled with diamonds. Look at that blue sky and the craggy mountains rising above the valley. It's a post-card. That's Eternity Springs down below, isn't it? I see Hummingbird Lake. Oh, wow. Your view is to die for."

"Appropriate, since murder paid for it."

"I'm jealous. Wonder how I could cook my way into a view like this? All I see out of my front window is a view of the house across the street."

He tossed the origami bird he'd just finished onto the pile of ornaments. "Do you ever think about moving home?"

"All the time. Especially in July and August when it's hot enough in Dallas to fry an egg on the sidewalk. My parents are growing older, and I'd like to be closer to them."

"You should move home and take over the Yellow Kitchen restaurant. Ali Timberlake told me just last week that she's ready to sell it and retire. You should think about it."

"Maybe I will."

He pushed his chair back from the table and rose to his feet. "Speaking of desserts...."

"I don't believe we were."

He shrugged. "We are now. Does your culinary repertoire include snow ice cream?"

Snow ice cream. A delighted smile stretched across Mary's face. "I haven't made snow ice cream in years."

"I think we deserve—"Nick broke off when his cell phone

rang. His expression brightened. He thumbed the green button and brought the phone to his ear. "Hey, buddy. What's happening?"

While father and son talked about the day's events at Disney, Mary tested her cookies and decided they'd cooled enough to decorate. She'd made her royal icing earlier. Since Nick didn't own any frosting tips, design options were limited. But the shades of red, green, and yellow that she'd achieved with her homemade food colorings pleased her. She proudly displayed the green icing to Nick, who dipped his thumb in the bowl and licked it. "Yum. That's delicious."

She scowled and wrapped his knuckles with her wooden spoon.

Nick winked at her and spoke to his son. "Cookie frosting. A friend and I are getting everything ready around here so that you and I can have Christmas when you come home. I know, Mikey. Michael, I mean. Christmas can come to Daddy's house after December twenty-fifth. Sure. I've cleared it with Santa Claus."

Listening to his son, Nick rose from the table. He sauntered over to the kitchen counter where Mary stood spreading green royal icing on sugar cookies shaped like Christmas trees. Nick snagged a cookie, and she rapped his knuckles a second time. "Stop that!"

CHAPTER 9

Nick wanted to laugh out loud. The realization startled him. It was the first time he could remember feeling this way since right after Thanksgiving when he received the court order regarding Mikey's Christmas visit with his mother.

"No, it's not Mr. Brick," he said, responding to his son's question. "She's a new friend I met yesterday. Her name is Mary Landry, but I call her Mary Christmas. Her parents live in Eternity Springs. She and her foster dog were on their way to visit when the blizzard hit, so they stayed here to be safe."

"A dog! What kind of dog, Daddy?"

"A mutt. A great big huge mutt."

"What is his name?"

"Her name. She's a girl. Her name is Angel, but I call her Frankenstein because she's the ugliest dog I've ever seen."

"Beauty challenged," Mary interjected.

Nick grinned. "She's fat, too, but that's cause she's going to have puppies before too much longer."

"Frankenstein! You talked about that yesterday. And she's

going to have puppies? I love puppies. What's a foster dog, Daddy?"

"Ah, well. See, my new friend Mary rescues dogs that don't have a family, and she helps them find their forever homes."

"So, Frankenstein doesn't have a family? That's so sad. Maybe we could be her family."

Nick's gaze settled on the ugly mutt. "She lives in Texas. She needs a Texas family."

He waited for the expected "Why?" but it didn't come. He was glad. It made him sound shallow to say he wanted a decent-looking dog if they were ever to get one.

"Is Angel still gonna be there when I get home?"

"Not at our house, no, but she might still be in Eternity Springs. Mary hasn't told me how long they're going to be in town. I'll tell her you would like to meet her dog, and we'll see if we can't find time to make it happen. Maybe she could join us for our Christmas morning. Would you like that?"

"I guess. Would Mary Christmas give me a present?"

"You mercenary you. Probably. She gives homemade gifts, so maybe she'll give you some cookies or something."

"I love cookies almost as much as puppies."

"Mary makes great cookies."

Mikey hesitated a moment, then asked, "Are you sure it's okay for me to have two Christmases, Daddy? Will Santa actually come twice?"

"Yes, in a way. A different way, but one I think you'll like."

"I don't understand."

"Don't worry about it. I'll explain it all when you come home."

"But we will have a Christmas tree and presents?"

"We will."

"What about my stocking? Will we put out cookies and milk for Santa the night before? I already gave you my present. Do I need to get another present for you for our second Christmas? I could buy something at Epcot today. I haven't spent all of my allowance that you gave me."

"I don't need a second gift."

"Is it okay if I give you one? I want to give you another present. I saw this space shuttle you'd really like. I have money."

Nick laughed. "Sure. You do what you want. But, seriously, don't worry about anything. Now, tell me what's on your agenda for this afternoon."

They spoke for another five minutes or so until Mikey's mother told him it was time to leave their hotel to return to the park. Nick disconnected the call and turned to Mary with a smile. "Want to help pick out a tree?"

"I'd love that. I have one more sheet of cookies to bake, though. Shall I do it first or after the harvest?"

"I need to shovel a path to the garage to get the equipment we'll need. Why don't you finish up here while I get everything ready?"

"Perfect."

Nick snagged another cookie, evaded her knuckle swat, and headed for the mudroom where he donned his snow gear. If he whistled "Joy to the World" beneath his breath as he removed his snow shovel from a storage closet, well, the Grinch police weren't going to come to arrest him or anything. And Mary Christmas might throw him a parade.

He might throw her a parade, Nick decided as he hit the garage door opener remote and stepped into the cold, the snow shovel resting on his shoulder. He owed her. Her gift of

Christmas cheer had the Santa Claus Killer well along the road to rehabilitation.

How sad that it had taken a snowbound sprite to show him the error of his ways. Why hadn't Nick thought to move Christmas to another day instead of picking up his sleigh bells and going home to hide?

Nick cleared off Frank's potty patch before working his way toward the garage. The snow was heavy and wet. Every shovelful felt like picking up a bucket of water. But the exercise felt good and helped to exorcise the last of his lingering moodiness.

It had been natural for Nick to sink into the darkness once again when he had dealings with Lauren. Hadn't that been his modus operandi when the marriage was failing? He'd dealt during that time by burying himself in murder.

Mikey had been his sole source of light. So, when his light flew off to Wallyworld, Nick's natural response was the Santa Claus Killer.

Then sparkle and sunshine knocked on his kitchen door in the middle of a snowstorm and chased away the gloom. Now the trick was to keep it at bay. How to manage that? How could he keep the light in his life once the elf no longer hung around his shelves? How could he keep the spirit of Christmas in his heart throughout the year?

Probably the first thing he needed to do was find some forgiveness in his heart where his ex was concerned. A big task, that. Nick wasn't sure his Grinch's heart had grown enough to accommodate forgiveness toward Lauren.

"Baby steps," he muttered to himself, his breath fogging in the cold mountain air. "One shovelful at a time."

Right now, he needed to concentrate on making a Christmas morning memory for Mikey.

Upon reaching the garage, he surveyed his power tools. How big a tree did he want? Hearing Mary's approach, he said, "We have a choice to make. What scale are we going for here? Big and beautiful or Charlie Brown or something in between?"

"Totally your call. Do you plan to supplement our origami ornaments with things you have stored?"

Ugh. That would entail unburying Santa from the attic, and he wasn't ready to face those ghosts of Christmas past. *Baby steps.* "I don't think so. I like this Christmas from scratch thing you've started."

"Then I'd shoot for more Charlie Brown than Rockefeller Center."

"I agree. I know just where to go. There's a stand of spruce I've been thinking of thinning out. It's close and easy to reach." He strapped his small chain saw onto the yellow utility sled, grabbed some straps, clippers, and rope. Then, handing Mary a lightweight bag, he added, "For pinecones or anything else you think we can use."

The hike took a little longer than he'd anticipated, primarily because Mary stopped every few minutes to exclaim about the view or the beauty of the afternoon or point out signs of wildlife. Her bag of treasures was bursting at the seams long before they reached their destination. Her joy and enthusiasm were contagious, and Nick found himself grinning like a kid at Christmas on more than one occasion.

He asked her to choose between five different trees, and after much debate, he fired up his chain saw and felled a nicely shaped blue spruce that stood a shade taller than his own six feet four inches. Mary prattled on about her wreath-making skills as she continued to forage for potential decorative supplies on the way back to the house. Her cheeks were rosy. Her big green eyes sparkled like twinkle lights. She was the picture of the Christmas cheer that she had promised and as sweet and appealing as her sugar cookie icing.

Nick spied the growth in the loblolly pine directly ahead. In this season of symbolism, he decided to take it as a sign.

Nicholas Carstairs halted beneath the mistletoe and pulled Mary Christmas into his arms.

CHAPTER 10

Santa Hunk has a killer of a kiss.

Mary had seen it coming, the speculative look in his eyes, intrigued, appreciative, and knowing. She didn't ward him off. She'd wanted this kiss from the moment she'd stumbled out of the snow and into his arms. The almost-kiss in his pantry only made the wanting worse.

Her eagle eyes had spied the mistletoe on their way out, and she'd been watching for it as they made their way back. She'd planned to try this same move herself, or at the very least ask him to stop and wait while she climbed the tree and harvested some for her goodie bag. She had mentally identified three good mistletoe hanging spots in his house.

When he'd stopped in the perfect spot beneath the tree, she'd had to swallow back a gleeful giggle. Great minds think alike, she decided just before his firm lips moving against hers sapped her ability to think.

He took his time with the kiss, and her lips sizzled with sensation. Nerves fired throughout her body, tightening her breasts, creating a powerful, hollow ache deep inside her. Her eyes were closed, her head thrown back. Surely the snow beneath her feet must be melting. Thank heavens he had a tight hold on her because she doubted her knees could hold her up. If she drowned in snowmelt, well, what a way to go.

When finally, minutes…maybe hours…later he released her, simultaneously numb and highly sensitized, she could do no more than stare up at him blankly.

"Merry Christmas," he murmured in a low, husky tone.

"Yes?"

He chuckled softly. "Not Mary with an A this time. Merry with an E." He pointed above them. "Mistletoe. Figured we shouldn't pass up the chance to spread some Christmas cheer."

"That was…uh…pretty cheery. Made me feel like I started hitting the wassail too hard."

"Funny. I feel like I have a really nice sugar buzz. I think we should harvest some of this for your bag. What do you think?"

Mary rolled her tongue around her mouth, still tasting him. What was he asking? What would she agree to if she said yes?

Did she want to sleep with Santa Hunk?

Oh, yeah.

Mary hadn't been with a man since Travis. She liked sex. She missed sex. She really, really, really, really would like to have sex with Nick Carstairs.

But she knew herself. She knew that in order to retain her self-respect, she needed more than just a physical release. As much as she enjoyed this lusty buzz, she couldn't give herself to a man unless her heart was involved.

So, it broke hers just a little bit to say, "I think a little mistletoe business can really brighten up a holiday. That said, I don't want any misunderstandings. I can only go so far with my gift of giving. I'm not a one-night stand kind of girl."

He tenderly stroked the pad of his thumb across her cheek. "Fair enough. I respect that. I respect you. Nothing wrong with drawing the line at mistletoe business."

Mary's heart lifted as anticipation sparkled through her. "In that case, get to clipping, Santa Claus."

He clipped enough mistletoe to hang in every doorway in the house. He also insisted on installing the cuttings and testing their effectiveness before putting up the tree.

The testing curled her toes. She liked this mistletoe business. If, by suppertime, the words 'magnetic North Pole' took on an entirely different meaning for Mary Christmas, who could blame her?

At eight-thirty, with her defenses weakened alarmingly, she retreated to the guest suite—alone. She tossed and turned but finally drifted off to sleep with visions of sugarplums—no, candy canes—one thick, hard candy cane, in particular, dancing in her head.

It's no wonder her mouth was watering and her pillow damp with drool when a large hand grasped her shoulder and shook her awake at ten thirty-seven.

"Mary, wake up. I have a surprise for you."

Santa Hunk. Christmas Eve. Peppermint North Poles. Mary's will was weak. "Good. I don't want to be good, for goodness sake."

"What?" Nick switched on the bedside lamp. Mary shielded her eyes as light assaulted her. He clicked his tongue, his gaze sweeping over her. "Oh, look at you. All rumpled and warm. You're adorable."

She blinked. "You're wearing a Santa hat."

"And a coat, too. Like it?"

"Why are you wearing a Santa costume?"

"You're gonna help me play Santa Claus. You're the merry elf."

"Roleplaying? Really? Now?"

"Well, there's a thought. I'd like nothing better than to get naughty with you, but that's not why I'm here. See, I couldn't sleep, so I put on a movie, and because I was thinking about you, I chose a Christmas movie."

"Die Hard 2?"

"No. I have an idea. A terrible idea. A wonderful, terrible idea."

"Awful," she corrected, recognizing the literary work he quoted.

"I need your help."

"I'm not going to help you steal Christmas, Grinch."

"No. Brush your hair and put your pompoms on, sugarplum, then come take a gander at what Frankenmax and I are doing in the basement. Be quick about it, though. We need to be wrapped by midnight."

"Frankenmax? What are we wrapping?"

"The Santa Claus Killer's Christmas pawdcast." He leaned down and kissed her quick and hard. "That's pawdcast with an 'a' and a 'w,' not an 'o.' The show drops at midnight every night. And this time, we're making an audio-visual production. A Christmas special, if you will."

As Nick turned to leave, Mary reached for his hand. To stop him? To pull him down into her bed? She'd never know for sure because at that moment, Angel rammed her way into the bedroom. Using her antlers.

Mary gaped. "What is that?"

"I adapted an old costume of Mikey's. It's papier mache."

"Why…oh." Finally, her sleep-muddled mind put it all together. Max was the name of the Grinch's dog. Nick couldn't find a reindeer, so he made one instead. And he recorded his podcast in his basement. He must be going to add a Christmas message to the episode that drops on Christmas Eve. "Has your heart grown three sizes?"

"Something has," he responded, giving a rueful glance down. Then a crash near Mary's bed had him quickly looking up. Angel had knocked the bedside clock from the nightstand. One of her antlers had broken and dangled in front of her eye. Nick said, "Well, shoot. Maybe I can tape it back together. If not, I at least got some good promo pictures."

"Promo for what?"

"We're gonna make Frank a star. Get dressed and meet us downstairs, and you'll see." Then he winked at Mary and left her bedroom whistling, "Santa Claus is Coming to Town."

CHAPTER 11

"IT'S TWENTY-FOUR HOURS UNTIL CHRISTMAS. WE HAVE A full plate of sugar cookies and half a carton of milk. It's dark out, and I'm wearing a Santa suit. Welcome to *What Was He Thinking?* I'm your host, Nicholas Carstairs. And tonight I'm inviting you to watch the show on our YouTube channel, because you're gonna want to see my special guest."

Nick leaned away from the mic and played the first few bars of the show's theme music, then segued into "You're a Mean One, Mr. Grinch."

"Regular listeners of this podcast will have tuned in to today's episode expecting a continuation of our series, the Twelve Murders at Christmas. That will continue tomorrow, but today we are switching gears a bit. You may have caught our recent episode with my former partner, Detective Dan Trevenios. During that show, I expressed my disgust with how crass and commercialized Christmas has become in our world today. Because of my rant and in keeping with the theme of this podcast, Detective Trevenios dubbed me the Santa Claus Killer."

He grinned past the camera at Mary, who stood in the

studio doorway. "I admit I embraced the title with pride. I owned it. I Scrooged and Grinched around happy as a reindeer in a birch forest. That all changed when a stranger knocked on my door seeking shelter from the storm, and Christmas blew into my world. Now, I want to share my story of the Santa Claus Killer killer. It begins, appropriately enough for this show, with a monster. Folks, meet Frankenstein."

He switched to camera number two, which was pointed toward the section of the studio where guests normally sat. There, Frank—sans antlers but sporting a red bow around her neck—lay sprawled on the forest green velvet couch.

With attention to timing and adding a comedic twist not ordinarily a part of his podcast, Nick told the story of Mary and Angel's arrival. He skipped over the parts where he'd been half-naked and lusting over more than her coffee and focused instead on the comfort and joy she'd offered. He spoke about her family's gift of giving to a stranger tradition.

"This evening," he continued, "I got to thinking about Mary's gift. I was curious about why her Christmas cheer managed to yank the Grinch out of me. Once I started being honest with myself, it didn't take me long to put my finger on it. While I ordinarily would rather have my molars yanked out with a pair of pliers, I decided to talk about it here tonight. After all, I'm late to the Christmas party. My opportunities to pay Mary's gift forward are limited by a ticking clock. So, listeners, fair warning. I'm going to bare my soul."

Nick paused and took a sip of liquid courage bourbon from a coffee mug. "We talk a lot on this podcast about what circumstances and influences create a killer. I'm here to tell you that the nexus of the Santa Claus Killer shares some characteristics with some of the psychos we study on this podcast. My rant about commercialism was an excuse. The fact was that before Mary Christmas stumbled into my heart and hearth, I was lonely. My loved ones aren't with me this year for Christmas. Lonely can take people down dark roads. That was me before the head Christmas cheerleader filled my home with the holidays."

He gazed at Mary, winked, and continued. "Here's where I'm going to pay this gift of giving forward. I know that loneliness isn't an isolated condition. There are lots of us out there feeling this way, especially around the holidays. Unfortunately, we're not all lucky enough to have a Mary Christmas blow in to blast the blues away. But—and here's the reason I'm doing this—Mary didn't arrive alone. She brought some medicine with her that is widely available. Too widely, in fact, which is part of the reason for this show. When we come back from break, I'll introduce you to tonight's special guests. You're listening to a Christmas Eve edition of 'What Was He Thinking?' with Nicholas Carstairs."

He pushed a key to play the music he'd prepared for the break, a mashup of his theme song, and dogs barking out Jingle Bells. Then he met Mary's gaze and smiled. "I take it you like my surprise?"

Her luminous green eyes glistened with tears. Delight filled her smile. "It's perfect. I'm so going to win the gift to a stranger show-and-tell."

"We're in it to win it. Now, I want to begin this next segment with a short discussion about the mental health benefits of pet ownership. Then let's segue into a conversation about rescue organizations and how their work helps both animals and adopters. I did some quick research on the mental health benefits of pet ownership and pulled some stats. Your personal twist on the rescue story makes it relatable. I think the audience will love it. We'll raise awareness, raise some money, and save some animals. I think the right message could reach some of those people who desperately need companionship, especially during this time of year. We plant a seed in the minds of people who haven't considered getting a pet or reaching out to a rescue."

"It's a great idea, Nick."

"So will you join me for the next segment?"

"Me? On camera? Oh, Nick. That's not...I can't. I wouldn't know what to say."

"I ask questions. You answer them. Nothing difficult. It'll be easy."

"I'm not wearing any makeup."

"You don't need makeup. You look great. You look beautiful, Mary. You *are* beautiful, inside and out." He glanced at the clock and noted the time. Then, approaching her, he lifted her hand to his lips and kissed her palm. "Tick tock. We need to finish this if I'm going to get both the video and the audio files edited and uploaded by midnight. So, what do you say, my little plum pudding? Will you share your story and help me give my gift to a stranger?"

Mary folded her arms, pursed her lips, and considered. "I will do it on one condition. You join my family for brunch Christmas Day and be part of our gift of giving tradition."

Nick gave her hand a squeeze. "I appreciate the sentiment, but that's a family event. I don't think it's my place to—"

"It's exactly the place you should be, doing exactly what you should be doing. So please, join my family Christmas morning, Nicholas. That's the deal."

He sighed and shrugged. "The Christmas family on Christmas morning? I guess I've asked for that, hmm?" When she grinned and nodded, he added, "I don't have to wear an ugly sweater, do I?"

"Not unless you want to. I could help you make one before the tow truck guy gets here."

Nick laughed and tugged her forward towards Frank's lounging couch. "Let's get this project finished before we begin another one, shall we?"

He got her settled in front of the camera and the mic, and moments later, began segment two by saying, "Welcome back to *What Was He Thinking?* Let me introduce you to my two extra special guests. This is Mary Landry, a professional chef and partner in Landry and Lawrence catering in Dallas, Texas. While I could do an entire show about her professional skills—her Irish stew is truly the best I've ever had—tonight, we are going to focus on her volunteer work for Wags and Walks Pet Rescue. Mary, welcome to the show."

"Thank you." As Mary spoke, the dog shifted her weight and plopped her head in Mary's lap. Mary tidied the bow Nick had fastened to Frank's collar and added, "Angel and I are delighted to be here."

"Angel," Nick rolled his tongue around his mouth, considered rolling out Frankenstein, and decided not to go there. "Let's dive in right there. Tell us about Angel, what breed of dog she is, and how she came into your life."

Mary began by describing her first meeting with Angel and by the time she started explaining how the foster and adoption procedures worked with Wags and Walks, she'd relaxed. Mary answered Nick's questions about rescue work easily and enthusiastically. In fact, she was so good and such a natural that Nick extended the segment beyond its ordinary period. He finally brought it to an end because Frank became a pest by nearly constant shifting and twisting on the sofa.

Nick returned to his usual seat behind a desk with Mary seated beside him for the third segment. Frank got down from the couch, and as the dog disappeared from the set, Mary asked, "Shall I bring her back?"

"No. Leave her be for now. We'll do a short wrap-up after this segment, and we can include her in it then."

Nick focused the third segment on mental health, the challenge of navigating the holidays while battling the blues, and how pets can help. He rolled out the research that he'd done earlier that evening before waking Mary. She supported his statistics with personal stories of things she'd witnessed in her rescue work. By the time he wrapped up the segment, Nick had decided that this might well be his best show ever.

"Maybe I should do a p-a-w *pawd*cast on an ongoing basis," he mused. "Maybe once a month or so. I'd enjoy it. I think we're gonna see a spectacular response to this show."

"I think so, too. It's an important topic."

He gestured toward his laptop. "You want to pull up the adoption application for Wags and Walks? Print a couple, and we can discuss the form during the wrap-up. I'll add a graphic at the end of the show when I do my edits, too."

"Perfect."

"While you're doing that, I'll go find Frank and bring her back. Want to end the show with one last appeal for an adopter for her? Bet this brings you some takers."

"Me, too. Angel will be famous."

While Mary went to work on the laptop, Nick went in search of the dog. He expected to find her in his home gym lying beneath the heater vent because it seemed to be a favorite spot. She wasn't there. He didn't locate her anywhere in the basement. Nor did he find her in any of her usual locations on the ground floor. "Hey, Frankenstein," he called. "Angel? C'mere girl."

He clapped his hands. Nothing.

Frowning, he climbed the stairs and first checked the guest room. Nothing. "Angel?" he called again, a little louder.

Still nothing.

"C'mon, you pain in the butt." Nick was running out of time. He checked his bedroom suite, then other rooms on the second floor, and when the dog still didn't appear, he retraced his steps to the basement and got methodical in his search.

He found her in the laundry room next to an overturned basket, lying on the pile of clean towels he hadn't found time to fold and put away. He took one look at her, did a double-take, and said, "Well now. Aren't you full of surprises?"

Making his way back to the set, he didn't know whether to grin or groan. Mary walked out of his office carrying the adoption application. "Where's Angel?"

"Change of plans with our wrap-up, Mary Christmas."

"Why is that?"

"Frank isn't interested, and we need to get this put to bed, or I'll miss my deadline. Ready?"

"Sure."

They took their seats, and Nick welcomed his audience back to the show. First, he asked Mary to go over the adoption application and review the process once again. Then he listed the Wags and Walks Rescue website address and promised to compile a list of recommended rescue groups which he'd add to his own website in the coming days. He also made a pitch for local animal shelters before transitioning into his closing thoughts.

"Thank you for hanging with us tonight as we took the show in this unexpected direction. If the lonelies are getting to you, I hope you'll reach out to a friend or for a four-legged one. Finally, I want to wish everyone a safe, happy, healthy holiday.

"Now, one last item before we tie a bow on this episode. I

had intended to bring Angel back on camera for our close and make one more appeal for a family to apply to give her a forever home. Turns out that Angel is otherwise occupied. Be watching for an epilogue of tonight's show to drop sometime in the next twenty-four to forty-eight hours. You're gonna love it, I'm certain. I'm Nicholas Carstairs, and you've been listening and/or watching the *What Was He Thinking?* Christmas Eve special. Merry Christmas!"

He played the closing music he'd prepared, the show's theme mashed up with "Rudolph the Red-Nosed Reindeer."

Frowning, Mary asked. "An epilogue, Nick?"

"Yeah. I expect it'll be a nice, short, little feel-good piece. Not what we'd planned for today, but I guess it's appropriate, being Christmas Eve and all."

"What is appropriate? And where is Angel?"

"Away in a laundry-room manger, my clean towels for a bed."

"Oh, dear. Angel got into your laundry?"

"Yep. Your dog is nesting. Merry Christmas, Mary. Frankenstein is about to give birth."

CHAPTER 12

MARY GAPED AND SHOOK HER HEAD. "NO, THAT'S impossible."

"Oh, it's possible. Trust me. It's happening."

"How do you know?"

"When I was a kid, our family dog had three litters. Also, my friend's German Shepard had pups in October. I was visiting when she went into labor, so it's pretty fresh in my mind. Frank is panting, nesting, and shivering. She's in labor."

"But it's too soon." Mary scrambled off the chair, ready to rush to Nick's laundry room. "It's too soon, and it's beyond the scope of my experience. I don't do puppies, especially premature puppies. Angel needs a vet."

"Well, it's the middle of the night on Christmas Eve. As long as everything appears to be going okay, I don't want to disturb our local veterinarian. Frank is going to have to make do with you and me. What delivery date did your vet give you?"

The question brought Mary up short. She didn't even

think about correcting his name use. Curse Rhonda Blankenship and the bikini she rode off with! "Actually, I never spoke to a vet about Angel. The woman who pulled her from the pound for Wags and Walks handled that. She told me Angel's due date is January tenth."

"Any chance she lied?"

The newlywed who supposedly ran away to Yap? For all Mary knew, she could have made up the entire elopement story just to rid herself of a difficult-to-place foster. "Maybe. I just don't know. Angel doesn't look like a dog who's ready to deliver."

"She's all coat. You can hardly see her belly for the long hair."

"True." Mary began hurrying toward the stairs, her mind spinning. Maybe Nick was wrong. Angel's appetite hadn't been good the past couple of days. "Perhaps she has a stomach virus. She could be sick, right?"

"She's in labor, Mary."

"I don't know what to do!"

"I do. Look, I'll be there to help as soon as I finish up here. Don't worry. I won't be long."

"Good. Okay. Thanks." Mary rushed to the laundry room, where she found Angel standing and pawing at a pile of towels. Nesting, just like Nick had described. The poor pup panted loudly. Was she in terrible pain? Then Angel turned in a circle twice before laying down on her left side.

"If I ever find myself in the South Pacific, I'm going to yip over to Yap and growl at that liar," Mary muttered.

Her Christmas holiday had just been turned on its head. It was almost midnight. Almost Christmas Eve. Was Mary going to miss Christmas after all? How long would this labor take? Could she move the puppies to her mother's house once they were born? How could she travel home with newborn puppies? What if the pups weren't full term and they died?

This was just shaping up to be the most snake-bit holiday trip ever.

Mary didn't know what to do. Should she call her Wags and Walks contact? Texas was an hour ahead of Colorado, which made it one a.m. there. Did she really want to wake someone up on Christmas Eve? What could they do?

Nothing. Nature was going to take its course.

Okay, then. She needed to calm down. She needed to think positive and act positive. "We've got this. What can I do to help you, Angel? Looks like you've chosen a decent place for this." Although, they needed to do something to protect the pups from getting wedged between the appliances. When Nick got here, she'd ask him for ideas.

What else? Did Angel need water? But hospitals didn't give water to laboring mothers. Or did they? Mary wasn't sure. She didn't know much more about having human babies than she did about dogs. "Don't require emergency treatment, Angel. Please."

In the end, Mary sat on the floor beside the dog. She stroked her, scratched her, and crooned soothing words to her. Mary had no clue about how the labor was progressing. She hadn't felt this helpless in a very long time.

Nick's approaching footsteps were a welcome sound. He entered the laundry with his arms full of a variety of items. "How is everything going here?"

"I don't have a clue."

"Courage, Mary Christmas. Frank and you and me, we've got this."

"Angel."

"All right. Since it's Christmas, I'll call her Angel."

Speaking to the dog, he said, "Sweet Angel mama. You've picked a good place for your whelping box, but I want to make a few adjustments to make everybody more comfortable. You probably can use a potty break, too. Mary, if you'll take her out, I'll add my hay to the manger and make things a little more comfortable in here."

"Okay. I can do that."

When she led Angel back indoors a short time later, Mary discovered that instrumental Christmas music played softly on the sound system. Lights in the house had been muted, while in the laundry room, Nick had created a box by blocking off the appliances with table leaves and making the fourth wall with the sled they'd used to haul the Christmas tree. He'd lined his laundry room floor with shower curtain liners, a comforter, and the towels that Angel had requisitioned. Off to one side sat rolls of paper towels and a box of latex gloves. Nick had moved floor pillows and blankets just outside the laundry door, and next to them, a wooden tray held a bottle of wine, two glasses, and a charcuterie board.

"You think of everything," she said as she guided Angel into the box.

"I try." Nick closed the "gate" and gestured toward the floor pillows. "Make yourself at home. This is liable to take a while."

Mary didn't make three circles before sitting down like the dog did, but she did take a minute to fluff the pillows and kick off her shoes. Nick sat beside her, poured them each a glass of cabernet, and asked, "Do you know Lori Timberlake?"

"The vet in Eternity Springs? My parents take their dog to her."

"We had a bit of good luck. A mutual friend who happened to be listening to the show took a flyer and texted her. She called me, and I gave her a rundown of our situation. She told me what to do and said to call her if we have any trouble."

"Oh, that's a relief."

"Her office isn't open tomorrow—well, I guess it's today now—but she'll meet us up there. They have room at their boarding facility for as long as you're in town."

"Oh." Mary closed her eyes leaned her head back against the wall. "That is a huge relief. Huge!"

"We can take Angel and her pups tomorrow. They'll take care of mama and the pups during your stay in town."

Mary slapped her hand to her heart. "It's a Christmas miracle. My mother would not be happy if I brought newborn puppies home on Christmas Eve, and I have no idea what kind of post-natal care that Angel would need." Then, prayerfully, Mary added, "Thank you, sweet little baby Jesus."

Nick handed her a glass of wine. He clinked their glasses in a toast. "To Christmas miracles."

"To Christmas miracles." She took a sip and lifted her glass for a new toast. "To Christmas pawdcasts."

"Here. Here."

"And sexy Santa Hunks who save elves in distress, has a soft heart for dogs, and kisses like the devil himself."

Nick laughed. Mary clinked their glasses, then polished off her wine and signaled for seconds. Nick kindly obliged.

Relieved, she relaxed. Relaxed, she grew excited about the pending event. As they settled down to wait, seated side by side, Nick's arm thrown casually around her, Mary asked him about his childhood pet, the mama of three litters of puppies. He told her about Pearl and her pups, and she talked about her beloved miniature longhaired dachshund, a spayed little girl named Sprinkle. "Sprinkle?" Nick asked.

"Had to be that or Tinkle. Peeingest dog you've ever seen."

They were into their second bottle of wine when the discussion moved from high school prom to bad college roommate experiences and on to memorable life firsts. Mary told him about the trauma of baking her first soufflée. She expected something similarly lighthearted when it was Nick's turn to speak. Instead, Nick talked about the night that his son was born.

"I wasn't happy about the pregnancy. The marriage was already rocky. I didn't think having a baby was the way to fix it. My wife made the decision for us both when she stopped her birth control pills and forgot to tell me."

Oh, Nick.

"I was not a supportive husband during those nine months, and that's on me. I wasn't ready to be a father, and I was so filled with righteous anger over her duplicity. I buried myself in work. Didn't go to doctor's appointments with her. We quit sharing a bed and a bedroom in the first trimester. I know I let her down in those months, and for that I take full responsibility. I could have done a lot better."

He closed his eyes and leaned his head against the wall. Mary snuggled up against him, silently offering comfort, as he cleared his throat and continued. "Her labor changed everything. She needed me. For the first time since she told me she was pregnant, we were a team. I did whatever she needed. I rubbed her back, held her hand, and helped her position the birthing ball. During her contractions, our gazes stayed locked. We had this laser force field thing going on. I was in it. We both were. It was as if each of those contractions got rid of some of the crap damaging our marriage. I remembered how much I loved her. I sensed a new beginning, and I was filled with hope and excitement."

He sighed and took a long sip of wine. "Then it all went to hell. She started hemorrhaging, the baby's heart rate plummeted. They wheeled her into the OR for an emergency C-section and told me to go put on scrubs and wash up."

Mary rested her hand on his thigh. "You didn't get to be with her during the birth?"

"No, I made it. Barely. I'll never forget that moment. The lights were really bright, and as I rushed into the room, the obstetrician pulled the baby out. He was all blue and had cottage cheese all over him. I was like, why is he blue? Do something! Then I saw him take his first breath, and he opened these huge, startled eyes and looked at me. There were half a dozen people in that room, and he looked at me first. Our gazes locked, and it was like it had been with my Lauren during the labor. I knew him. We knew each other. Boom. I was in love."

Tears stung Mary's eyes. Had she not already been just a little bit in love with Nick, that would have tipped the scale.

Nick released another heavy sigh. "Looking back, I think we might have been all right had it not been for the C-section. Lauren had a horrible recovery. She didn't bond with Mikey like she should have—no fault of her own because it took all her energy to function. Taking care of the baby fell to me. Those first few months are a blur. I use exhaustion as my excuse for missing the signs."

When he didn't continue right away, Mary asked, "Postpartum depression?"

"Yep. That and painkiller dependence. By the time I figured it out, my wife was hooked. I tried to help her. Managed to get her into rehab once, but…" Nick shrugged. "She left us. Figuratively first, then literally. She found another guy willing to help her get what she wanted the most

—pills and alcohol. We divorced, and Mikey and I moved to Eternity Springs."

Mary's heart ached for Nick and his son. For his ex-wife, too. Yet, there remained one question unanswered. "She's better now?"

"Supposedly. Lauren jumped through a lot of legal hoops to earn this time with our son. Letting him leave with her last week was one of the hardest things I've ever done."

Wrapped up in his story, Nick and Mary lost track of events occurring inside the laundry room, so the little squeaking sound coming from inside surprised them both. "Oh…oh…oh! Angel has had a puppy. Nick. Look. Oh, my. We are terrible midwives."

Angel was licking the puppy fiercely. Nick rose, donned and pair of gloves, and stepped over the makeshift barrier to assess the situation. "All looks well," he said a moment later. "Good job, Mama. Sure looks like a full-term pup to me. Do you know what breed of dog Angel mated with?"

"Haven't a clue."

"Well, the pup's coat will be lighter in color once she's good and dry. She's a little ball of gold."

"A girl, then?"

"Yep."

"A girl." Mary clapped her hands and bobbed up and down on her tiptoes like a teenaged girl at a boy band concert. "A healthy little girl. How wonderful. Way to go, Angel. She needs a name. What should we name her? Something Christmassy since it's Christmas Eve."

"How about Frankincense?" Nick suggested. "After her mother."

Mary rolled her eyes and dubbed the first pup Noelle.

The rest of the litter arrived relatively quickly. By the time Mary dragged herself off to bed a little after three a.m., five new little Angels had joined Wags and Walks Rescue's available-for-adoption roll.

When Nick checked his email Christmas Eve morning shortly after nine, one thousand seven hundred twenty-two adoption applications were in his inbox. He forwarded one thousand seven hundred twenty-three applications to Mary Christmas.

CHAPTER 13

Notice that Christmas was ruined arrived when the phone rang at eleven seventeen a.m..

Nick answered his cell as Mary pulled from the oven the cookies she'd made to give to the wrecker driver. Moments later, he factually relayed the news.

The snowplow assigned to clear one of the main roads between Eternity Springs and Nick's place had broken down a short way from town. Parts weren't readily available. The plows deployed in other directions wouldn't be able to take up the slack.

The bottom line, Mary realized, was that she wouldn't make it home in time for the Christmas Eve festivities.

She tried to be an adult about it. She truly did. She straightened her spine, squared her shoulders, and reminded herself of all of the things for which she had to be thankful. Yet, despite her best efforts, her smile grew shaky and moisture pooled in her eyes. A lone tear escaped and slid down her cheek.

"Stop that," Nick said, using the pad of his thumb to wipe it away. "You are breaking my heart."

"I'm such a baby, I know."

"There's a Shakespeare quote that's applicable here. 'Though she be but little, she is fierce.' You are the strongest elf I know. If you had to miss Christmas, you would deal."

"I know. You're right. I need to listen to my own sermon, don't I? I preached to you the idea that Christmas does not always need to happen on December twenty-fifth. I'll get to Eternity Springs eventually. My family can enjoy a second Christmas, too, just like you and Mikey."

"Yes, well, you also climbed on your high reindeer about the magic of Christmas. Maybe you ought to hang your pointy elf hat on that, sugarplum. Tap the heels of Mikey's red slippers together three times and say 'There's no place like home.'"

"I don't think you got enough sleep, Nicholas. The Wizard of Oz is way out of season."

"I don't have time to sleep. It's Christmas Eve, and I'm Santa Claus. If you'll excuse me, I have some prep work to do. While I'm doing that, I'd like you to make fresh coffee. You'll find a large thermos in the cabinet above the fridge. Fill it up, would you? And then take Angel out to do her business. Leave your outdoor gear on afterward."

Mary realized she kind of missed him calling her Frank. "Are we going out?"

"That's the plan." He put his hands around her waist, lifted her off the floor, and kissed her mouth with a loud smack. "The Santa Claus Killer is dead. Long live Santa. You created this, Mary. Now you need to believe."

"Where are you going?"

"Where else? I have to hitch up my sleigh."

"What sleigh?"

"I have an errand to run on the snowmobile. I should be

back in half an hour or so. Then it's over the river and through the woods to grandmother's house we'll go."

"What? We're getting out? How?"

"Believe, Mary Christmas. You need to believe."

Twenty-five minutes later, she heard the hum of an engine close by. She crossed to one of the front windows, and her jaw dropped. "Oh, holy night. He wasn't kidding."

He drove an enormous red truck with a snowplow attached to the front.

She rushed outside and was there to meet him as he switched off the engine and climbed down from the cab. "How the heck did you manage this?"

"Let me tell you a little secret about podcasts, Mary Christmas. We have a lot of fans who drive long hours for a living and listen to pass the time. That includes truckers, delivery drivers and *snow plow operators*—and they're some of the best people on earth. I put out a call for help, and one of my fans delivered. Ain't she a beauty?"

"She's the most beautiful thing I've ever seen."

"Check out her name. It's here on the back panel."

Nick brushed away some muddy snow to reveal a name painted in glittering gold letters. Mary read it and started to laugh. "I guess we need to refer to her as a he from now on."

"No," Nick corrected. "She is a girl. Santa's reindeer are all girls."

"No way!"

"Yes way. Male reindeer shed their antlers in early December."

"I didn't know that."

"You mean I knew something about Christmas that Mary Christmas didn't know? Well, ho ho ho."

A short time later, with Angel and her pups comfy and

snug in their backseat bed, Mary Christmas and Santa Hunk set off for town in Rudolf the bright red snowplow, a flashing beacon light guiding the way.

CHAPTER 14

THEY ARRIVED IN ETERNITY SPRINGS WITHOUT INCIDENT AND took Frank and the pups directly to the vet's boarding facility, where Lori awaited them. Following a quick but thorough examination, the veterinarian declared mama and fur babies healthy and promised they'd be well cared for until Mary was ready for them. With the dogs tended to, Nick took Mary Christmas home. "Finally!" she exclaimed as he pulled their train to a stop in front of the Landry family abode.

People poured from the house. In short order, he met Mary's entire family. Her father pumped his hand, clapped his shoulder, and thanked him profusely. Her mother—a lovely older version of Mary-rushed him with a hug and cried and laughed and emoted all over him. Her siblings and their spouses also expressed their thanks and gratitude.

The Landry's made Santa jokes as they helped unload the sleigh and raved about last night's show, about which they'd apparently fielded calls all morning. Once the sleigh was unloaded, the Landry's insisted he come inside.

Nick gently refused the invitation. "I didn't get much

sleep last night, and I'll be honest, I need a nap. But I'll see you all at Celeste's a little later."

Earlier Nick had told Mary that he'd booked a room at a guest resort called Angel's Rest Healing Center and Spa. After more than a decade in business, Angel's Rest attracted visitors from all around the country, even the world. Thanks in no small part to the owner, the wise and beloved town matriarch, Celeste Blessing. She also hosted an annual holiday party at Angel's Rest that wasn't to be missed, and he and Mary had agreed to meet there later.

"And he's coming over for brunch tomorrow, too," Mary told her family.

She sparkled and bubbled with happiness. Nick badly wanted to kiss her, but he settled for squeezing her hand. "See you later, Mary Christmas."

"See you later, Santa Hunk."

He frowned slightly at that, then gave his head a little shake. "Do me a little favor if you get a chance this afternoon?"

"Of course. Anything."

"Check your email."

With a wave, he departed and a short time later checked in at Angel's Rest. When he was shown to a cozy two-bedroom cabin, he wasn't the least bit surprised to find it decked out for Christmas, complete with a decorated tree. The theme of the decorations was a blend of Santa and angels. No surprise, there. That's how Celeste Blessing rolled.

Nick took a long, hot shower, ate the sandwiches Mary had packed and included with their coffee, then dove into bed and fell immediately asleep.

It was glorious. If Nick's arms felt just a little empty without an elf on the shelf of his chest, well, little boys didn't get everything they wanted for Christmas. But, of course, he hadn't anticipated so much as a lump of coal until Mary and Frank upended his holiday.

The one gray spot in his day was that he'd yet to talk to Mikey. Nick had missed the boy's call during the trip down to town. The voicemail his son had left made his heart twist. "I'm sorry I didn't get to talk to you now, but that's okay. I have a surprise for you, Daddy. A big surprise. You're gonna love it. Merry Christmas!"

Nick made sure the volume on his phone was turned up high as he tucked his cell into the pocket of the black slacks he'd brought to wear to Celeste's party. Then he pulled on a solid red cable-knit sweater, combed his silver hair, and debated trimming his beard, but no. This was Christmas Eve. Based on past experience, half the people he spoke to tonight would crack some sort of Santa joke. He might as well own it. He might as well rock it. With any luck, he'd have his own Christmas elf at his side.

"Mary Christmas," he murmured, staring at his reflection in the full-length mirror in his bedroom. Maybe he'd look into making a trip to Texas in February. He could do Cupid as well as Santa Claus. All he needed was a banner and his birthday suit. His name might be Nicholas, but he was no saint. Grinning wickedly, Nick left the electric candles burning in the cabin windows and made his way up to the Victorian mansion where tonight's party was being held.

Already, the place was packed. The sounds of merriment and laughter rose to the rafters. Each room had a Christmas tree with old-fashioned bubble lights and ornaments galore. The scents of cinnamon and spruce swirled in the air. Angel decorations of one sort of another were everywhere one looked.

Nick's Christmas podcast was the talk of the party. Reviews were flattering, and everyone liked that he'd made

Mary and her foster dog stars. When asked if he intended to do a follow-up starring the puppies, he confirmed that was his plan.

Nick wandered throughout the mansion, keeping an eye out for his elf. The only one he spied was the little doll tucked up high on a shelf in the breakfast parlor. The elf on the shelf that Mikey would call James sat perched atop a figurine of a dog that had an astonishing resemblance to Frank, sans the scar. The theme of this room was the Twelve Dogs of Christmas, and that was where Mary found Nick about fifteen minutes after he'd arrived.

She greeted him with a shocked exclamation. "One thousand seven hundred twenty-three adoption applications!"

He grinned at her. "Did you read them all?"

"No, of course not." She paused and added a twinkle to her eyes as she explained, "No need to read past the first."

"So, I passed? I'm approved?"

"Oh, I approve of you, all right. How could I not? Obviously, this entire thing was Christmas magic at work. Congratulations, Mr. Carstairs. Angel has found her forever home with you."

"Frank."

Mary sighed heavily, though her green eyes twinkled. "Frank."

"And one of her pups for Michael?"

"And one of her pups for your son."

"Awesome. C'mere. There's something I want to show you." He steered her toward the center of the room and jerked his thumb upward to where mistletoe hung. Then, in front of her parents, Celeste, what seemed like half of Eternity Springs, and the Twelve dogs of Christmas, Nicholas Carstairs kissed his Mary Christmas quite thoroughly.

Then an unexpected, familiar voice broke through the haze of his desire. "Daddy, who is that lady you are kissing?"

Nick released Mary as if she were made of fire. Which she sort of was. He whipped his head around toward the voice. "Mikey? Mikey!"

"Surprise, Daddy! This is our surprise. Mom brought me home early so that we can spend Christmas with you! Miss Celeste says Santa will be able to find me at cabin number four."

Shocked speechless, Nick looked past his son to where his ex-wife hovered in the doorway. She wore a hopeful but uncertain smile. "If that is okay with you, Nick?"

It took a moment for him to put a name on the emotion flooding his heart since he'd never expected to experience it. Forgiveness.

"Yes. Definitely yes. It's more than okay with me." Christmas with Mikey. "Thank you, Lauren."

His ex-wife's smile went from hesitant to healing, and Nick shared the feeling. Until alarm washed through him. "I don't have your presents with me, Mike." Nick felt Mary slip her hand into his and squeeze it, and he thought of the puppies. "Not all of them. I do have one. I have your big present."

"You have my big present?" Mikey exclaimed. "Seriously? You didn't know I was coming home! How did you know to bring it?"

"Christmas magic," Nick repeated. Then, tearing his gaze away from his son, he gazed down at the woman beside him. "A little elf dropped by the house and taught me to believe in the magic of Christmas."

On Christmas morning, with some Santa assistance by Eternity Springs' vet and the Landry family, Mikey found a puppy beneath his Christmas tree. Since it was Jesus's birthday, he named the little boy dog King. Nick, Mikey, and Lauren attended church together on Christmas morning and called at the Landry home afterward for brunch.

Over quiche and fresh fruit and melt-in-your-mouth delicious cinnamon rolls, each of the Landry's and Nick presented their tale of Christmas giving to those assembled.

Voting wasn't even close. One thousand seven hundred twenty-three adoption applications won running away, all of which were forwarded to Wags and Walks Rescue to pair up prospective adopters with homeless pups. Mary Christmas vowed to win next year. Santa Hunk declared he'd be going for two wins in a row. The following year, the family gathered at Nick and Mary's house for the Christmas morning tradition.

And so ends the story of how Mary Christmas's gift of giving slayed the Santa Claus Killer using the magical weapon of elf dust, puppies, and love.

BETTER THAN A BOX OF CHOCOLATES

AN EXCERPT

Chapter One

Dallas, Texas

Ali Lovejoy cruised along I30 headed west in her sweet little Mercedes convertible listening to classic rock on the car stereo. Hoping to catch a traffic report as she headed home toward Fort Worth, she sang along with The Boss until the final notes of "Born To Run" faded into an all-too-familiar jingle. Then, quick as a rattlesnake, she struck the preset button to change the station before the teddy bear advertisement blared from her speakers.

"…send lovely red roses, delivery guaranteed…."

Her index finger poked again.

"…delicious chocolate-covered strawberries and …."

Jab.

"…peek-a-boo pajamas to your Valentine today!"

This time, Ali hit the "off" button. She'd rather risk bumper-to-bumper traffic than listen to one more of those commercials.

Not that she had anything against stuffed animals or

flowers or sexy lingerie or chocolate anything, because she didn't. In fact, Ali was a big fan of romance.

It paid the bills.

Ali made her living as a wedding photographer. This very moment she was on her way home from signing a lucrative contract with a MOB—aka mother-of-the-bride—to photograph all of the events surrounding her daughter's June nuptials.

Romance was good for Ali's bottom line.

Valentine's Day made her cranky.

The day of red hearts and roses had been a source of trouble for her for much of her life, from Kindergarten's decorated shoeboxes to last year's one-for-the-record-books humiliating Valentine's Day. Now, during this first week of February, all she wanted to do was play Rip Van Winkle and hide under the covers until February 17th.

She tacked on a few extra days to allow bargain shoppers to clear the shelves of discounted chocolates, which was a real sacrifice because Ali did adore her chocolate.

The touch screen on her dashboard signaled an incoming call. Recognizing the number, Ali smiled as she answered. "Jessica! Well? Was the shopping trip a success? Did you say yes to a dress?"

"No!" Her best friend and college roommate replied with a groan in her voice. "I found some 'maybes,' but nothing that screamed 'This is the one.' My mom is getting frustrated with me."

"I can't imagine why. You've only tried on, what? Six hundred wedding gowns?"

Jessica sniffed. "No more than five hundred fifty."

"Well, no rush. You still have plenty of time."

"Speaking of time, that's why I'm calling. I have a huge favor to ask."

Uh oh. If Jessica Martingale said it was a big favor, it would be a big favor, and Ali would be obligated to grant it. After all, if not for Jessica going above and beyond when Ali came down with mononucleosis during their last semester at the University of Texas, Ali wouldn't have graduated on time. And her friend had been her rock many other times since.

Her friend continued. "Ordinarily, I wouldn't dream of suggesting this because it's a huge ask. But under the circumstances, I think it could be a win/win for both of us. Sean will be happy because a relative of his is pushing for it. Something to do with a distant, elderly aunt. I admit I don't understand that part, but the Gallaghers are a huge family, and I haven't met everyone. Of course, I'll understand if you can't do it, and my feelings won't be hurt or anything. I just want it to be you so bad because you're the best photographer in the entire world, and you're my maid of honor, and we could have a really fun long weekend."

"Jessica. Jessica. Slow down. I gather you want me to photograph something? That's not a big ask."

"I haven't told you the who, what, where, and when."

Ali waited. And waited. And waited. "Jessica?"

She asked in a rush. "Will you come to Colorado and photograph the reenactment of my Christmas Eve engagement?"

"You jerk!" Ali exclaimed, slamming on her brakes to avoid hitting the florist delivery van that abruptly changed lanes in front of her.

"Oh."

Hearing the hurt in her former roomie's voice, Ali quickly explained. "Not you, goose. I was talking to the idiotic driver in front of me. Of course I'll take your engagement photos. I'd be honored, in fact. The problem is my schedule. You know I work almost every weekend."

"That's the 'when' part. I know you aren't working this particular weekend because you've sworn a blood oath that you're not leaving your house."

Oh. Ali's stomach sank. She knew what was coming.

Jessica continued, "This year, Valentine's Day falls on a Saturday. So we're doing the reenactment on Valentine's weekend."

Okay, that is a big ask.

Ali had spent the past twelve months padding a lawyer's bank account while she put the pieces of her heart back together. Approaching the first anniversary of the death of her dreams on the worst day of the year was bad enough. The last thing she wanted or needed was to risk running into her Valentine's Nightmare Past. But unfortunately, the way her luck ran, that's precisely what would happen.

And yet, this was Jessica doing the asking, and the venue was a small, isolated mountain town in Colorado. The odds of running into her ex in Eternity Springs were next to nil, and she could still follow through with her current Valentine's evening plans from there. So doing this favor for her bestie wouldn't break her vow in any way. In fact, it might be good to get out of the house.

"Cool. I'm free on Valentine's weekend. I can watch horror movies on the night of the fourteenth in a hotel room as easily as I can in my own bedroom."

"Horror movies? You don't watch horror movies."

"It's a new tradition of mine I've decided to establish in keeping with the spirit of the holiday."

Jessica laughed. "Oh, Ali. You're a mess. Well, we will be staying at Sean's family's bed-and-breakfast in Eternity Springs. They might have a theater room. If you're serious about this new tradition, I'll reserve it for you. I've been warned that we need to make reservations for everything we want to do while we're in town because there's a hot air balloon festival that weekend, and the place is packed."

Ali's artistic interest perked up. She tried to recall what Jessica had told her about the place where she'd gotten engaged. She had a mental vision of a Victorian snow village, and the hot air balloons didn't fit it. "I'm intrigued. Isn't there a lake in this little town?"

"Yes. Hummingbird Lake. I think the balloons take off from there."

"Cool. That's something I'd like to watch if we have time."

"You'll definitely have time. The balloon flights take place at dawn. It won't be interfering with anything I have scheduled."

Ali laughed at that little truth. Jessica was not a morning person. The two women discussed their travel schedules until Ali heard an electronic sound in the call's background. Jessica said, "Gotta go. Class is about to start."

"Go whip those Kindergarteners into shape, Miss Martingale."

"I'll try. I swear this year's group is five going on twenty-five. I'll email you the deets about your reservation at Aspenglow Place B&B. Bye!"

"Aspenglow Place B&B," Ali repeated softly as she checked her mirrors and switched lanes. Didn't that sound inviting? And a winter balloon festival—bet she could get some glorious shots. She hadn't done any outdoor photography in way too long. It'd be a nice change.

And so, to Ali's complete and utter amazement, she found herself looking forward to the second weekend in February. The drive to her destination from her home in Fort Worth could be made in one long, hard day of driving, but she preferred to get an early start and break it into two.

The trip required using her work vehicle, a four-wheel-drive SUV with plenty of storage space for all of her equipment. So, the night before her departure, she loaded the SUV, then set her alarm for Zero-Dark-Thirty and crawled into bed.

Ali dreamed about drinking Earl Gray tea with a tiny, elderly woman who had crystalline blue eyes and the lilt of Ireland in her voice.

Weird.

CHAPTER 2

Eternity Springs, Colorado

Max Romano peeked through his office blinds and gazed down into the tasting room at the Tipsy Angel Microbrewery. "What are all these people doing here? All these women!"

Lying at his feet, Barney, his coal-black Newfoundland and best friend, thumped his tail twice.

"It's a Thursday in February!" Max continued. "We should have one customer, two at the most. And they should be locals!"

Max's sister, Gabriella Romano Brogan, propped her long legs atop his desk and crossed them at the ankles. With her right hand, she idly scratched her own Newfoundland, Bismarck, behind the ears. Gabi's brilliant blue eyes gleamed with amusement as she observed, "That's a terrible attitude for a business owner, brother dear."

"Yeah, well. You try walking around Eternity Springs in my shoes for the past week or so."

"You mean because of the rumor floating around that our famous cousin, Luscious Lorenzo, is in town? That's why you asked me to take Barney on a walk with Bismarck instead of walking him yourself, isn't it? You're afraid to show your pretty face around town?"

"It's not fear. It's self-preservation. And I'm not pretty."

Gabi giggled-snorted. "Sure, you're not."

Max scowled over his shoulder at his sister. "I'm glad you think this is so funny. I'm not the only person catching flack, by the way. Flynn needs to stay on his guard. You've told me women find that eyepatch he wears sexy."

At the mention of her husband, Gabi's laughter died. She yanked her feet off the desk and sat up straight. "Did somebody bother Flynn?"

"Not that I know of, but I'm afraid it's just a matter of time. The crazies went after Cicero yesterday."

"Cicero! Why? What happened? He didn't say anything to me."

"He was probably afraid you'd pull out your old sheriff's uniform and go looking for the free-handed floozies yourself."

"Free-handed floozies? What is this, the 1930's?"

"One of them ripped my shirt! Another went for my junk."

"Seriously? Okay, start at the beginning, Max."

"Fine." Barney's tail gave a hard thump against the floor in support. Max continued. "Cicero and I met for coffee at the Mocha Moose and stood in line next to some people who are in town with the balloon festival. They didn't believe me when I denied I was Lorenzo, and Cicero thought it would be cute to stir the pot, and he joked around."

"I mean, as far as jokes go, it's actually pretty clever."

"Not helpful." He scowled. "Anyway, before you know it, these three women have us backed up against the wall. And then two of them come at me trying to manhandle me! It wasn't a pleasant situation."

"Oh, dear."

"Yeah. So, that's why I asked you to walk Barney for me this morning. Even with a mountain of a dog at my side, I'm wary of showing my face in public right now."

Disgust lacing her voice, Gabi wondered, "What is wrong with people? I know Lorenzo's the star of a number one Netflix series, but is that really enough reason for people to lose their minds?"

"I blame social media for everything. Anyway, I also need you to call Lorenzo and convince him that he needs to get splashy for the paparazzi. I don't care where he is. He needs to draw the heat away from Eternity Springs. I would call him, but he'd go to ground just out of spite. You always had more influence with Lorenzo than I did."

"That's because I didn't break his nose when he was twelve."

"He deserved the punch. He knows it. Come on, Gabi. I'm begging you. You have to convince him to do this. Remind him that he owes us."

It was true. Lorenzo Romano owed his Hollywood career to the Eternity Springs branch of the family.

"I can try, I guess," Gabi said, though her voice was riddled with doubt. "If he's laying low, he has a reason. You know he's never been one to dodge the limelight."

"That's true. It has me a little worried, to be honest. It's why I called in the big guns—you."

Gabi's reply was interrupted by the pounding of boots on the stairs and then the rap of knuckles on his office threshold. "Sorry, boss, but we have a rush. Things are really backing up. Could I get a little help?"

"Sure, I'll be right down." Max grimaced and groaned. "You don't happen to have a disguise tucked away in your backpack, do you? Maybe a wig or a fake mustache?"

"Sorry, left my wig and fake mustache at home today." Gabi unfolded herself from the chair and stood. "But I do have a little time. So I'll sub for you."

"And you'll call our cousin?"

She sighed. "Yes."

"Thank you, Sis. I'll owe you."

"Yes, you absolutely will, and I'll collect. I know just how I'll do it, too."

"How's that?"

A secretive smile formed on her sister's lips. Then, lightly, she said, "You'll find out soon. Maybe Sunday during the family gathering at Aspenglow Place."

"Oh, man. I forgot," Max said, wincing. His maternal great-grandmother, whom the family called Nonnie, had scheduled a long weekend's visit with her granddaughter, their mother, at her home in Eternity Springs. As a result, the four Romano siblings and their families were all invited— actually, commanded—to gather for Sunday dinner at widowed Maggie Romano's B&B. "This Lorenzo business has me completely off my game. I told the Callahans I'd go skiing with them on Sunday."

"You'd better call and cancel. Mom and Nonnie would take turns having your hide if you didn't show for dinner."

"True, that. I'll be there. I wouldn't miss a family dinner with Nonnie for the world." He waited for a beat and added, "I'd be afraid she'd put a curse on me."

"She'd do it, too," Gabi agreed. The Romano siblings shared a smile. "Speaking of Nonnie, maybe you should ask for her help with Lorenzo."

Max considered the idea. A native of Ireland, Nonnie had claimed to be in her eighties for at least the last twenty years. Her insight was credited for everything from the basis of the

California branch of the Gallagher family's fortune—she had advocated a stock purchase after a grocery-store conversation with Walt Disney's housekeeper—to the New York branch of the family's success with their pub. And when it came to romance, well, one ignored Nonnie's advice at one's own peril.

"I don't know. Nonnie is impossible to predict. She might not take my side. When is she arriving in town?"

"Tomorrow afternoon, I believe. You know Lorenzo will do whatever Nonnie tells him to do."

"That's true." Lorenzo was a believer, a convert, if you will, to the notion that Nonnie had been gifted with "The Sight." Lorenzo was one of three Romano cousins who'd had their tea leaves read during the festivities surrounding Gabi's wedding, and her predictions led him to move out to LA to pursue an acting career.

Eighteen months later, he was cast in the glitz-and-glamor binge hit *Riviera.* The rest, as they say, was history—a historical pain in Max's ass.

"Tell you what. Call Lorenzo today, and see what he says. If he doesn't cooperate, I'll talk to Nonnie in person tomorrow and try to convince her to drop a GMOAB on our cousin."

"GMOAB?"

"Grandmother of all bombs."

Gabi laughed. "So, what will you do in the meantime? Close the Tipsy Angel? Stay home and play video games?"

"Hey, I'm about to beat the zombie lord. As far as work goes, I'll call Celeste at the Angel's Rest Inn and see if any of her employees can cover for me here at the tasting room for a couple of days. If I have to go out, I'll go with a crowd. I'll wear a hat and sunglasses everywhere."

"Sounds like a plan. I'll phone Lorenzo this afternoon."

"You're awesome, Sis." Max leaned over and kissed her cheek.

"I know." Gabi blew on her knuckles and polished them against her shoulder. Then she winked and added, "Now, I'd better get out there and help John before he throws in his bar towel and quits."

Max's heart was lighter than it had been in days as he took a seat behind his desk and placed a call to his good friend and Eternity Spring's most beloved citizen, Celeste Blessing.

Once they had exchanged greetings, she said, "This is quite the coincidence. I was just about to call you. I have a favor to ask of a man with muscle, so I thought of you."

"Uh oh. Did I mention I just threw out my back?"

She laughed at his obvious joke. "I need someone strong to put up the decorations tomorrow at Mistletoe Mine. We'll be recreating our Holiday Walking Tour display from this past Christmas, including the Beloved Chamber. Aaron planned to do it for me, but he truly did tweak his back."

"Oh, no. Not too bad, I hope."

"No, he says he's fine, but I can tell he's sore. He'll be fine after a few soaks in our therapeutic hot springs. I'm proposing that he fill in for you at the Tipsy Angel while you're at Mistletoe Mine. As far as that goes, all of the decorations are in storage on site. The work doesn't involve a lot of back and forth, but it is plenty of heavy lifting. Is there any chance you would do this for us?"

"I would love to do heavy lifting at Mistletoe Mine tomorrow. You're the answer to a prayer, Celeste."

"Yes, well, I do try."

So, that was how Max found himself in Mistletoe Mine the following morning armed with keys, a crowbar, plans, and schematics for the electrical parts of the display, along with his toolbox and his work gloves.

Three years ago, when the Eternity Springs Historical Society decided to create a Holiday Walking Tour as a fundraising project, the cavern on Angel's Rest Healing Center and Spa property naturally became the event's highlight stop. The cavern was a magical natural wonder, a labyrinth of chambers filled with glittering stalactites hanging like icicles from the ceilings and majestic stalagmites rising from the floors. Illuminated and decorated for the holiday season, the cavern was a fascinating fairyland that filled visitors with awe. As an added inducement to support the cause, every ticket buyer received a chance to win the Walking Tour's Grand Prize—a night at the Mine Shack, the resort's unique and luxurious apartment, which included a secluded hot springs grotto.

Max spent the day hauling, lifting, and hanging. He decked the halls and jingled the bells. He hammered, screwed, and when the situation warranted, he didn't hesitate to let loose a good solid kick.

Celeste structured her decorations around the theme "Tunnel of Love." The decorations included painted plywood backdrops, artificial trees, music, mannequins, stuffed animals, and angels. Lots and lots and lots of angels. Max hung lights, draped garland, and dangled ornaments. He climbed a ladder about seven thousand times, and he was oh-so-glad to do it.

Long ago, while watching his brother Lucca attempt to deal with the spotlight as a pro basketball player, Max had decided he valued his privacy more than fame or fortune. That's one reason why life in Eternity Springs suited him so well. He really didn't appreciate Lorenzo Romano getting famous and screwing it up for him.

Fangirls gave him the shivers. And not the good kind, either.

Better Than A Box of Chocolates

On sale January 12, 2023

Read on for an excerpt from the third Celebrate Eternity Springs novella, THE SUMMER MELT.

THE SUMMER MELT

AN EXCERPT

Chapter One

Something cold and wet landed on Dana Delaney's hands as she unlocked the back door of Scoops, her ice cream parlor in Eternity Springs, Colorado. Glancing above her, she grimaced. Snowflakes? Seriously? It was the seventeenth of May!

"Double Chocolate Toffee Crunch," she muttered, cursing in her own particular way. Nothing like springtime in the Rockies.

It might just send her to the poorhouse.

She stepped inside her shop, flipped on the lights, and stowed her purse and lunch tote in her office. Glancing at the wall clock, she read eleven fifty-one. She had nine minutes to complete the short list of daily tasks required before opening the store.

Not that she needed to worry about a rush of customers at noon. Oh, she would see her handful of daily customers, but unfortunately, this type of weather didn't bring in tourists and townspeople the way sunshine and warm weather did.

She needed sunshine and warm weather and tourists this summer. Lots of tourists. Lots and lots and lots of tourists.

Dana sighed heavily and went about her prep. She opened the front door at three minutes to noon and carried her broom outside to sweep off the sidewalk. An occasional snowflake continued to swirl in the gusty breeze. As she bent to sweep debris into her dustpan, a familiar voice called her name. Dana straightened and smiled to see her friend, Celeste Blessing, crossing Spruce Street from the Mocha Moose, holding a lidded paper cup in each hand.

Celeste was the owner of Angel's Rest Healing Center and Spa. Now a thriving resort, Angel's Rest had breathed new life into Eternity Springs when the small mountain town was in danger of dying. Celeste was exceedingly kind, beyond generous, and wise in ways that benefited all those who requested her counsel and advice. She had become the town's happiness ambassador. For Dana, Celeste filled the hole created by the passing of Dana's beloved mother and maternal grandmother.

Today, just like most days, Celeste sparkled. She wore a matching gold rain jacket and hat over skinny jeans. Her light blue eyes gleamed from beneath the wide-brimmed rain hat that sat jauntily atop her short, silver-gray hair. Her smile made the overcast day seem brighter. "Happy Tuesday, Dana," she said. "Do you have a few minutes for a cup of tea and a chat? I have a business proposition for you."

"I absolutely have time." Only a fool would be too busy to listen to a business proposition from Celeste Blessing. The woman had uncanny instincts.

Chimes jingled as Dana opened the door and gestured for her friend to proceed her into the shop. Celeste took a seat at one of the half dozen red-and-white-striped parlor sets that served as seating inside Scoops. After dumping the contents of her dustpan and stowing her broom, Dana joined her.

"I guess it's more a favor than a proposition," Celeste began, scooting one of the paper cups across the table toward Dana. "It's about one of my summer employees. Have you met Rusk Buchanan?"

The name sounded vaguely familiar to Dana, but she couldn't place him. "I don't believe so."

"He's one of my study abroad students."

Then it clicked. The Colorado Rockies teemed with international students during the summer. "Oh, is he the guy that the teens in town are calling the 'Hot Scot'? I overheard the high school cheerleading team talking about him when they stopped in for ice cream last week. He's in one of the college programs but he's got the high school girls in a tizzy."

"That's him." Celeste sipped her tea, nodded, and sighed. "He's a sweetheart and an excellent worker. I hired him to lifeguard at the resort swimming pool, but it's not working out. Yesterday alone, we had three incidents of false cougar drownings."

Dana frowned. "False cougar drownings?"

"It's not just the high school girls who are in a tizzy. Females at least a decade older than Rusk who go into the pool—where the water is still quite chilly, mind you—and pretend to struggle to be rescued by a wet 'Hot Scot.'"

"Oh." Dana couldn't help but chuckle. "Oh, dear."

"Yes, oh dear. And that's only the older women. Once school lets out and the summer tourist season begins in earnest, my fear is that the swimming pool will be overrun. I don't want to have to close it to locals or institute a lottery system for daily entrance."

"That would be a shame." The Angel's Rest swimming

pool was the only public pool in town, and it's where the majority of the children in Eternity Springs learned to swim.

"It's quite the conundrum. I would shift Rusk into a different job at the resort, except that would leave me short one lifeguard, and it's late in the season to be finding someone qualified."

"That's true," Dana agreed. Eternity Springs was a geographically isolated small town. Finding help was always a problem. Finding specialized help could be a nightmare.

"I have thought of one possible solution, but it involves you. So that's where the favor comes in."

Dana knew what Celeste was about to say, and her stomach sank. "You want to poach my assistant manager."

When Dana opened Scoops four years ago, Alissa Cooper had been sixteen and her first hire. She was intelligent, dependable, and trustworthy. She'd been a godsend for Dana.

She also was a certified lifeguard.

Celeste held up her hand, palm out. "Not poach. Hear me out, Dana. I know how much you count on Alissa. What I'm proposing is a trade. Rusk for Alissa. Of course, they'd both need to agree to the change, but based on comments Rusk has made, I feel confident he'd be on board. I didn't want to approach Alissa before I spoke to you. However, I suspect she'd like the job. You know how much she loves our pool. Last summer, she swam laps almost every morning before work."

It was true. Alissa would love to spend her summer outdoors. However, Dana identified one insurmountable problem. Grimacing, she said, "Oh, Celeste. I can't match Angel's Rest's pay scale."

Especially not this year, she thought, what with the bank loan she'd taken out last fall she had coming due at summer's end.

Dana wasn't getting wealthy with her ice cream parlor, but she made a decent living from it. And, she loved the lifestyle Eternity Springs offered. Ordinarily, she could withstand a year of bad weather. However, last fall she'd chosen to make a substantial donation to help with medical expenses for her oldest and dearest friend's seven-year-old son. Dana didn't regret incurring the debt for a minute, even if it did mean she had to sweat snowfall in May. Seven-year-old Logan Ellison had received his new kidney and was doing great.

"No worries, there. Angel's Rest will cover the difference. However, I don't think you've grasped the big picture, Dana. Think about it. Cougars eat ice cream, too."

"Oh. *Cougars.*" Dana sat back in her chair. The beginnings of a smile flickered on her mouth as she gazed through the shop's large picture frame window to the dreary, overcast afternoon. "Even when it's chilly, you think?"

Celeste's blue eyes twinkled over the cup she brought to her mouth for a sip of tea. "I have a hunch that Scoops will have a banner season with Rusk serving up dips of Royal Gorgeous Gumdrop."

"Okay then. I know better than to bet against one of your hunches. I'll talk to Alissa when she comes in. I'd also like to visit with your study abroad student."

"I anticipated that. I invited Rusk to stop in for an ice cream cone at twelve twenty."

Dana glanced at the clock on the wall and read twelve seventeen just as a tall, broad figure strode past the front window. "Celeste, you are a wonder."

The door's bells chimed, and a young man stepped inside. He nodded toward Celeste, then met Dana's gaze and smiled. *Whoa. Hot Scot, indeed.*

Rusk Buchanan was the very cliché of tall, dark and handsome, and his smile had enough wicked in it to tempt any female with a pulse. So, when his heavy-lidded green eyes focused on Dana, she instinctively wanted to preen—until he called her ma'am during the introductions.

"It put me in my place," Dana explained to her friend Amy Elkins when they met for a happy-hour drink after work.

"And reminded me that he's barely old enough to buy me a drink! He's an awfully cute fella though. If a Hollywood scout ever discovered him, he could easily be America's next heartthrob."

Rusk started work at Scoops the following day. By week's end and despite the lingering cold spell, Dana's daily sales had tripled. The young man quickly proved to be a collegiate champion flirt while working behind the safety barrier provided by the display case.

Warmer weather finally arrived and settled in with Memorial Day Weekend. Dana extended operating hours from nine to nine. Rusk worked the day shift, and Dana regularly arrived in the morning to find a line outside the door.

As the days ticked by, Dana worked long hours, stepping up production to keep up with demand, happy as a clam to be doing it. She had yet to begin dating again following the breakup of a longtime relationship last year, so putting in extra time at Scoops suited her perfectly. At the close of business each day, she made a silent toast to Celeste when she counted her receipts. If sales continued at this pace, she'd have her loan paid off by the Fourth of July.

Everything changed the second week of June when her phone rang at eight a.m. and Rusk Buchanan whispered, "Dana, I am unwell. I will not make my shift today."

"Oh, no! What's the matter?"

"I think the fairies came calling while I slept. They drove

over me with a truck, banged my head with a hammer, and scraped my throat raw with a zester."

"Oh, Rusk. I'm so sorry. Do you have a fever?"

"No, but I do have a strange rash on my belly. I'm to see the doctor in a wee bit. I am sorry to leave you in the lurch."

"Don't worry about that." Though Dana couldn't help but have a flutter of concern. She'd had a horrible sore throat, fatigue, and a rash when she had mononucleosis in college. The illness put her down for the count for three whole weeks. "Follow the doctor's orders and concentrate on taking care of yourself. Get well soon, Rusk."

"I'll do my best. I will miss my daily dairy fix."

Dana decided she wasn't about to let her Highland Hottie do without. Arriving at Scoops early, she packed a half dozen pints of his favorite flavor and headed for his address, a garage apartment that Celeste provided at one of her rental properties. Dana climbed the wooden staircase to the apartment above the garage and knocked on the door. "Rusk? Special delivery. Pike's Peach is guaranteed to tickle your tastebuds and soothe your sore—"

The door swung open, and an invisible mule kicked the air right out of Dana's lungs. Because a stranger wearing nothing but gym shorts, sneakers, and sweat stood gazing at her with a curious look.

"Throat," Dana croaked. Actually, abs. A sculpted six-pack of them, covered by a light dusting of hair that arrowed downward to disappear into his shorts. And, *whoa,* she jerked her gaze upward, but it got stuck on shoulders. She'd always had a thing for broad shoulders on a man, and his spanned an area as wide as the front range of the Rockies.

He wasn't Rusk. He was a bigger, brawnier version of Rusk. An older version of Rusk.

Dana's new employee spoke of his family often. This

must be his older brother, the former professional baseball player who had moved to Florida to live with their grandparents during high school. He now made his living as a highly successful sports agent. His name was Cal, she believed. Short for Calum.

Oh, wow. This Buchanan man was definitely old enough to buy her a drink.

Dana got a taste of the Hot Scot hormone rush that had tripled Scoops' sales so far this summer. Her heartbeat fluttered like a hummingbird's wings.

And that was before the slow, sexy smile softened his chiseled jawline, and his dark green eyes gave her an appreciative once over. Her mouth went dry.

Then he spoke. "May I help you?"

Hearing a faint echo of Rusk's Scottish burr emerge from Cal Buchanan's mouth spiked the temperature of the heat flushing through her. She feared her Pike's Peach might just melt all over the landing.

Wordlessly, she held up the basket.

His gaze focused on the ice cream pints in the basket she carried. Those gorgeous green eyes lit with pleasure, and Even Hotter Scot said, "Ah. You must be Dana Delicious."

THE SUMMER MELT
On sale June 1, 2023

ALSO BY EMILY MARCH

REUNION PASS

CHRISTMAS IN ETERNITY SPRINGS

A STARDANCE SUMMER

THE FIRST KISS OF SPRING

THE CHRISTMAS WISHING TREE

The Eternity Springs: McBrides of Texas Trilogy

JACKSON

TUCKER

BOONE

Celebrate Eternity Springs Novella Collection

THE CHRISTMAS PAWDCAST novella

BETTER THAN A BOX OF CHOCOLATES novella

THE SUMMER MELT novella

And, SEASON OF SISTERS, a stand alone women's fiction novel.

The Bad Luck Wedding Historical Romance Series

THE BAD LUCK WEDDING DRESS

THE BAD LUCK WEDDING CAKE

Bad Luck Abroad Trilogy

SIMMER ALL NIGHT

SIZZLE ALL DAY

THE BAD LUCK WEDDING NIGHT

Bad Luck Brides Quartet

HER BODYGUARD

HER SCOUNDREL

HER OUTLAW

THE LONER

Stand Alone Historical Romances

THE TEXAN'S BRIDE

CAPTURE THE NIGHT

THE SCOUNDREL'S BRIDE

THE WEDDING RANSOM

THE COWBOY'S RUNAWAY BRIDE

ABOUT THE AUTHOR

Emily March is the *New York Times, Publishers Weekly*, and *USA Today* bestselling author of over forty novels, including the critically acclaimed Eternity Springs series. Publishers Weekly calls March a "master of delightful banter," and her heartwarming, emotionally charged stories have been named to Best of the Year lists by *Publishers Weekly, Library Journal,* and Romance Writers of America. A graduate of Texas A&M University, Emily is an avid fan of Aggie sports and her recipe for jalapeño relish has made her a tailgating legend.

Emily invites you to register for her newsletter at www.EmilyMarch.com/newsletter

Made in the USA
Monee, IL
11 December 2022